YOUR ROBOT DOG WILL DIE

Also by Arin Greenwood

Save the Enemy

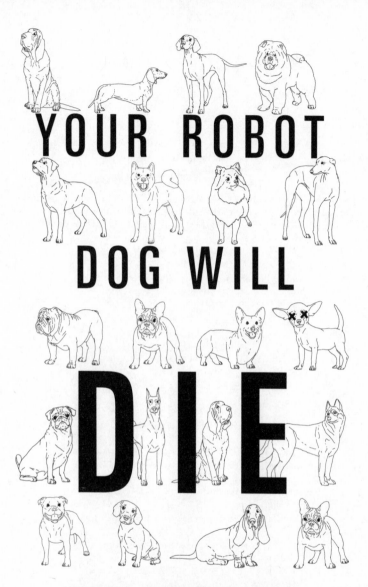

YOUR ROBOT
DOG WILL
DIE

ARIN GREENWOOD

SOHO
TEEN

Published in the United States by Soho Teen
an imprint of
Soho Press, Inc.
853 Broadway
New York, NY 10003

Library of Congress Cataloging-in-Publication Data
Greenwood, Arin
Your robot dog will die / Arin Greenwood.

ISBN 978-1-61695-852-7
eISBN 978-1-61695-840-4

1. Dogs—Fiction. 2. Robots—Fiction. 3. Best friends—Fiction.
4. Friendship—Fiction. 5. Dating (Social customs)—Fiction. 6. Missing
persons—Fiction. 7. Islands—Fiction. 8. Science fiction. I. Title
PZ7.G85286 You 2018 DDC [Fic]—dc23 2017026486

Interior design by Janine Agro, Soho Press, Inc.

Printed in the United States of America

10 9 8 7 6 5 4 3 2 1

*For my beloved husband Ray and
our house full of black and white animals*

YOUR ROBOT DOG WILL DIE

Dogs! Don't you love them? Don't you wish you could live with them still? Friends, we are very excited to tell you that you can!

The Organics may no longer be with us, but the scientists at Mechanical Tail have spent many years and millions of dollars perfecting the next best thing: robot dogs!

Did we say the next best thing? In some ways, our robot dogs are even BETTER! Our robot dogs are the same as Organics—they'll walk with you, they'll play fetch, they'll even wag their tails! (Remember that?) But all without any risk or danger or vet bills!

I've never gotten used to the rep from Mechanical Tail showing up once a year to replace my robot dog with a new one.

As always, it's a cheerful girl wearing a turquoise-blue Mechanical Tail polo. Her tag says "Rain." Maybe it's her name, or maybe it's an order to the universe. Rain! No more drought!

She stoops down to my eye level—I'm on the floor, holding Derrick—and tells me in a chipper voice: "You're going to love this year's dog *so much*."

I'm bawling, my arms around Derrick. He's little and orange and white. I've spent the previous year walking him, playing with him, talking to him. Loving him. I think the other Dog Islanders have developed thicker skins, harder hearts. We all go through this once a year, every year. I know it's coming, but it hurts so much every time.

"Is that really your name? *Rain*?" I ask. I want to make her feel bad and to put off what is coming.

She nods. "Yes," she says. "Hippie parents. Idealistic. They thought if they gave me the name, it might help end the drought." She smiles. She has cute dimples. I really resent this fact.

"Yeah, that really worked," I say, sarcastically. Though, actually, the drought has been easing up a little lately, thank Dog. But *Rain* must be thirty or forty years old, so I can't imagine her stupid name had anything to do with it.

"Where did you grow up?" I ask. Stall. Stall. Stall.

"California," Rain tells me. "I went to engineering school. Then I got my dream job at Mechanical Tail. And now here we are."

"This is your dream job?" I ask her. "Taking away my best friend? Killing him."

"Oh my Dog. I put that so badly. I apologize, dear. But don't you know how special you are? You're so special. That's why you are trusted with these different robot dogs instead of just being stuck with the ones the normal kids have to buy in the store," Rain says to me. "You are blessed to have this special opportunity."

Yes, of course, I do feel special—I know that we are very special, living here, with the world's last real dogs, all six of them, as well as the world's newest robot dog models. I've spent my whole life here. I know how lucky I am to be one of just a few dozen households with the privilege of being an integral and permanent part of this community. I'm one of just three kids. Three *remaining* kids.

Sure, lucky. Right now I feel devastated though. Every single time, this is how I feel. This is my fourth go-around. This is my fourth time being crushed. And that's just counting my own *personal* robot dogs. My family's had, and lost, others as well. Like we had the one that wasn't very fun or friendly but was supposed to be able to wash dishes with its tongue. (That function didn't work very well; it was one of the last times Mechanical Tail went for a practical robot dog instead of one that served as a companion.)

Honestly, even losing that one was hard and I don't even remember its name. But not like this. Not like Derrick. They really perfected the model this time in terms of making me love the hell out of a piece of machinery.

"Please let me keep him," I cry, knowing it's futile but having to say the words all the same. "I promise. I'll take good care of him. I won't tell anyone. You won't miss him, you're going to kill him anyway!"

"I can't," says Rain. It's what the reps always say. "I'm sorry. You're going to love your new dog. I swear. And you're performing an important public service, Nano Miller. The world is a better place because of your sacrifice. A kinder place. You will never forget David."

"Derrick!" I shout.

"Forgive me," she says. "I practiced saying the right name all the way here. I wanted to make this easy for you, Nano. I'm so sorry. You'll never forget *Derrick*. And we will never forget what you did, which helps us make sure no flesh-and-blood animal will ever suffer again. Thank you, Nano."

I am crying so hard my head hurts. My tears and snot are getting Derrick's fur wet. The fur doesn't react well to dampness. It clumps in a distinctly unnatural sort of way.

"Come here, boy," the rep says to Derrick.

He looks up at her with those trusting eyes (*programmed* to look trusting; I know this, I know this, I know this is true). He licks my cheek ever so delicately and walks to her.

She pats him on the head and says, "Good robot dog."

Derrick wags his tail. It's a little jerky, the wag. That part hasn't been perfected yet. Still, I love it.

"Do you want to say goodbye?" the rep, Rain—*Rain,* what a stupid name, what a stupid person—asks me and my mom.

Dad has decamped to the designated Parents' Room, where he can shut the door and no one is even allowed to knock, except Mom, and then only if it's an emergency. He and his robot bartender will be having some intense one-on-one time.

I think Dad imagines this space as his own private tiki bar. Mom and Dad used to go to a tiki bar in Rhode Island before they moved to Dog Island. It was called East Greenwich Eden. They sometimes still talk about it, wondering if their favorite bartender, Raymie, is there behind the bar slinging punch bowls after all these years.

Actually, the Parents' Room has got a terrible couch that Mom won't let Dad keep in any *public* part of the house. The couch was left behind by another family that left back fifteen years ago or so. It has cup holders. Mom finds the cup holders "really visually offensive." But the Parents' Room is just for comfort and privacy. And a water-free rum punch, made by a bow-tie-wearing robot, from powder and chemical slurry.

Maybe Dad's in the Parents' Room now having a drink because he doesn't much care that my robot dog is dying. Maybe after this many times he doesn't care anymore. Or maybe he's decamped to the Parents' Room because it's too hard for him to be here for this terrible ritual, again.

Mom stands over me. She has a look on her face that I can't quite read. Somewhere between pain and pride, with a dash of distractedness.

I grab Derrick in my arms again and kiss the top of his head. I tell my robot dog I love him. I thank him for being my robot dog, this past year. For being such a good boy, even if he's got no choice in the matter; it's all programmed in. His programmers did a good job.

"Thank you," I whisper in his little pointy ear. "Thank you. I love you. Thank you."

The rep reaches under Derrick's belly as I am holding him. She's about to press the button that will make Derrick shut down.

I've been through this four times now. I know how it goes. His eyes will go dark. There will be quiet. You don't even realize the robot dogs are making any kind of constant white noise, until the sound is gone.

And now it's gone.

Mom rubs her eyes.

"Goodbye, friend," I say one more time to what is now just a thing. Derrick is a shell now. Wet "fur" and no life.

The Mechanical Tail lady whistles. She smiles so big as the new dog walks into the room, eyes bright, tail up. The tail seems to have been given an upgrade. This new one's face seems more engaged, more Organic. He's got brown fur, brown eyes, and a big blocky head that makes him a little scary looking. One ear is up, the other down, which is cute. His fur is obviously softer. Looks more like hair than nylon or whatever it is they used on my Derrick.

"This model is designed to bond strongly with one person. For owners who don't like their robot dogs being too indiscriminately friendly," says Rain. *Rain.* My Dog, what a stupid name. "Plus, it has certain vocal abilities and a couple of new safety features. I hope you will enjoy it."

The robot dog wags its tail slowly back and forth as it looks around the room, taking it all in: me, my mom, the sky blue walls, the old shabby wicker furniture. Mom prefers shabbiness with a touch of cool over comfort with cup holders.

The robot dog walks over to me and sits down. Raises one paw.

"It wants to shake your hand," says the rep. "You're the one it will bond with."

I don't take the paw. I resolve to stay hard this time. Not to let myself care for the machine. At least not so much that I can't say goodbye without it hurting so much.

The dog looks at me with a quizzical expression. It then lies down and rolls over to show its belly, its tongue lolling out the side of its mouth. I don't rub the belly.

"Let me show you," Rain says, bending down and stroking the new robot dog's stomach. It shakes its hind leg while she gives a scratch. Derrick didn't have that feature. Rain smiles at me as if I'm supposed to be *amazed.* I am kind of amazed; I start to cry again. I miss Derrick and I'm already betraying him.

"I thought it was only going to bond with me," I say.

"This isn't bonding. It's just a belly rub. It's more for me than for him—it," Rain says. "What are you going to name this guy?"

There is only one name that seems possible: Billy, for my brother. And a year from now, I will lose this Billy as well. Maybe if I steel myself right, this one will be easier.

CHAPTER 1

Wolf, Jack, and I are sitting on the sand at the beach. It's just past sunset. You can still see a little bit of the sunset's pink-and-orangeyness over the horizon, while the rest of the sky is now a smoky gray.

The sand feels cool on my hands and toes but the air is finally warm; the Florida version of winter is winding down. This year the "winter" lasted four whole weeks. Longer than last year. I don't like the cold. But on the other hand, every day we're below 85 degrees feels like a little more reassurance that the drought won't come back.

We all grew up here at the sanctuary. The only three kids who are still here. We've been sitting in this same place, on this same beach, basically, for all our lives. What's new—newish, at least—is that Wolf's hand is just grazing mine. It makes me feel like my whole body is submerged in a warm bath and that everything around me is a little muffled or something. It's kind of embarrassing how his hand touching mine conjures the memory of what a warm bath feels like, given how many years it's been since I have had one. I get the occasional "real" shower, using actual water, but mostly I just wipe myself down with those smelly Sani-Fresh pads once or twice a day. Wolf smells the same, though. We all do.

Wolf. Wolf with floppy, curly brown hair. Wolf, who is kind of short, but so am I, so who cares. His small nose. His big eyes. Hazel. They're hazel, "with rings of gold around the hazel," Wolf likes to say, batting his long eyelashes. A group of long-time residents who call themselves the "Bad Bitches of Dog Island" always say those eyelashes are wasted on Wolf.

I like them. "Don't I have beautiful eyes?" he asks me. He stares into my eyes. My mud-brown eyes. No gold rings.

This thing with Wolf is recent and thrilling and unexpected. It's also making Jack act really weird. He keeps grunting and refusing to look at us and making passive-aggressive comments at his robot Chihuahua, Mr. Chi-Chi Pants.

"Mr. Chi-Chi Pants," says Jack, looking into his robot dog's face. "Do you think anyone here is being extremely rude?"

Jack, whose black hair is always a little bit stiff and crinkly because of this gel that his mother rubs into his head every day. Jack wears the same Dog Island clothes that we do—stiff shorts, old T-shirts, all in materials that don't need washing with water, that can be blow-cleaned—looks different than me and Wolf. He somehow looks like he's going to go off to the office soon. He just gives off an impression of profession-alism and no-nonsense-ness.

We, of course, have no offices here on Dog Island. We have plenty of nonsense. I'd like to have more nonsense with Wolf right now, in fact. He and I start to gaze into each other's faces once more.

Mr. Chi-Chi Pants doesn't say anything. He's an old model, pre-speech. (He's also not really a he. The robot dogs aren't gendered per se, but you invariably end up using pronouns that correspond to the names you give them.)

Wolf can speak but is choosing not to, I guess. Jack takes the last hit of weed, carefully stubs out the joint and slips it into his pocket. He never litters.

I just run my fingers through the sand, feel how soft it is, how cool compared to the warmth of Wolf's skin.

With my free hand I toss a ball to Billy. He catches it, brings it back, panting heavily and thumping his tail. He yips until I throw the ball again.

"Okay," I tell him. "Okay, Billy. Hold your horses."

"He doesn't have any horses," says Wolf. "Who even has horses anymore?"

"Want to go robot horse riding next weekend?" I ask.

There's a small "stable" of old-fashioned robot horse models that the three of us muck around with sometimes. These are some very old Mechanical Tail prototypes. They were supposed to replace "real" horses—the Organics—out in the real world so as to minimize or eliminate the cruelty we humans inflict on these magnificent creatures. No more hideous carriage rides. No more punishingly cruel horse racing. And so on.

Except the Mechanical Tail versions never caught on. They didn't run fast enough to replace Organics at the track. No one liked a robot horse-pulled carriage ride through Central Park in New York City. There was nothing "romantic" about that, apparently.

Plus, the robot horses kept breaking. Ours are broken and rusted, too, but since Wolf has been apprenticing with the Dog Island handymen and handywomen, he's learned how to tinker with them enough to get them walking a few steps every now and then. And that's pretty fun. Plus it helps to fill the day.

"Sure," Wolf says. "Jack, you coming robot horse riding?"

Jack grunts. Billy whines softly. Then something catches his attention. He lifts his front paw to point. I didn't know he had that function. I pull out my phone, which is on a chain around my neck, tucked under my shirt, and unfurl the flexible, rolled up screen to press the "positive interaction" button, so the Mechanical Tail robot dog developers will be able to tell that I enjoyed what Billy just did, in their quest to build the perfect robot pet. Then I follow Billy's paw with my eyes.

A cat, just strutting along by the water. I squint; I can't tell if it's a real cat or one of the robot cats from this distance, and I don't want to get up.

"Go get it, Billy," I say.

Billy dashes over the sand toward the cat and picks it up by the scruff of its neck. He trots back over to the bench and puts the cat down in front of me, wagging his tail. Its tail. His tail. He's Billy now, already.

"Good boy," I say, pressing the "positive interaction" button again. I feel a twinge of guilt. I remember pressing the button for positive interactions with Derrick all the time at first, but then I got used to him and it dropped off. I only gave him one negative interaction that I remember.

It was when he accidentally got wet, after I'd had him a few months—and then his tail wagged against my leg and gave me a small shock. That wasn't his fault, though. I shouldn't have pressed the button.

Billy wags his tail even harder. It's hard not to love Billy. (Which is, of course, the whole point.) It's hard to remember that he will be taken from me, a year from now, to stay cold inside. That *it* will be taken away.

I lean forward to look at the cat more closely. Wolf moves his hand to the top of my back, just below my hair. My cold insides get warmer. My face feels hot; I'm sure I'm turning red. Luckily, it's almost dark out and the beach lights haven't come on yet.

The robot cats have gotten so realistic it's getting hard to tell them apart from Dog Island's few remaining Organic cats anymore. It's really just in the eyes now, where you can see a bit of difference. A robot cat's eyes are just a wee bit brighter. Of course if you look closely at its tummy, you can see the belly button spot where it gets recharged every month or so.

Solar-powered robot cats would make more sense in Florida, of course. But they wouldn't work so well in Michigan, or Russia, or Rhode Island. And the robot cats are being developed as a sort of insurance, in case what happened to the dogs happens to other animals as well. It won't take so long to replace the Organics, if Dog forbid, it's necessary to do so. In that case they will have to be dispersed around the world, same as the robot dogs.

"Robot, right?" I say.

"Yeah," says Jack. He pushes back his brown hair with one

hand and grimaces. "Nothing real here. No need to call in the authorities."

I squint at Jack. He sounds bitter. He sounds bitter a lot lately.

"Hey," says Wolf. "What gives?"

"Nothing," Jack says. He stands up and slides his feet into his paw protectors—that's what we call flip-flops—without even brushing the sand off first. Still, not looking at us, he says, "I'm going home."

"Be safe," Wolf calls out, as Jack shuffles across the beach, holding Mr. Chi-Chi Pants with one hand and raising the other. He makes a very aggressively hostile gesture with one of his fingers. Wolf laughs.

"That guy," he says. Then he picks up my hand again. "This girl," he mumbles. My heart starts pounding. If there were a button for "positive interaction" with Wolf I'd have broken it by now.

Wolf leans in to kiss me. His lips are soft. We start to lean back, start to lie down. My fingers in his soft hair. His hand on my hip, my waist, even my boobs, which have gotten mortifyingly prominent recently. The world disappears. Nothing exists, except for this, except for us.

Except for: "Nano. Nano Miller. Please come home for dinner, Nano Miller."

This order comes in Mom's voice through the speakers in Billy's mouth. He's dropped the ball and his mouth just hangs open the whole time that he/Mom are speaking. I really, really hate this new "human speech" feature. The old model just sounded like a *dog* when it "spoke." This is really creepy. Plus embarrassing!

"Okay!" I shout at Billy while pressing the "negative inter-action" button on my phone several times. At least this model can't hear what you're saying or broadcast it. This is more like a radio, not a phone. At least for now. I'm sure we'll be getting that function soon enough. Well, unless enough people like me complain. Why can't they just keep the dogs dog-like?

"You can invite Wolf and Jack if you'd like," says Mom, through Billy's mouth.

I look at Wolf. "You want to come over?" I ask.

"I wish I could," he says. "Judy and Peter need me at home." Wolf calls his parents by their first names. That isn't more or less common than any other way of addressing the people who created you, on Dog Island, since Jack, Wolf, and I are currently the only kids here. Jack only has a mom, and he calls her Mom.

Billy gives me a stare that seems very meaningful. I wonder if Mom is somehow directing him to make that look. He might just want me to throw the ball again. Alterna-tively, he might just be having an electrical glitch in his "brain."

"I'm leaving!" I say, getting up. I brush off my feet before putting my sandals back on but feel too embarrassed to brush off my butt and back and hair.

Billy wags his robot tail. It's a bit jerky. I'll add a note about the jerky tail to my notes for Mechanical Tail. Maybe I will add a note about jerky Mom, too.

"I'll walk you home," Wolf says.

He takes my hand. Billy picks up the ball and walks along-side us. Wolf grabs the ball from Billy's mouth, tosses it. Billy does nothing. I run up the street and get the ball, then throw it half a block. Billy runs after the ball, gets it, brings it back, sticks his mouth to my free hand until I take the ball and lob it on down the street again.

I guess I like that Billy only likes me. I don't get why robot dogs like chasing balls. It feels manipulative. They aren't Organic Labrador retrievers.

It's about a mile walk, over those pretty brick streets and not-as-pretty cracked sidewalks. We stroll, not talking. Just calling out "Heya!" and "Shalom!" and "Dog be with you!" to the occasional other Dog Island residents we see out along the way. We have this wonderful multitude of ways of saying hello. *Heya* to those we know well. *Shalom* to the newcomers or people we are a little formal with. *Dog be with you* to anyone who's achieved some amount of, I don't really know how to say it, *holiness* here. You just know who you have to say it to.

I, like, can't think of anything to say to Wolf right now. It's making me a little anxious, honestly. Wolf and I didn't have any trouble finding topics of conversation before. Being quiet wasn't any trouble then, either.

"So, are your parents all kinds of worked up about tomorrow?" I finally ask. Marky Barky is coming for a visit, which sets the grown-ups into a tizzy.

Marky Barky is our nickname for movie star Mark Mooney, Dog Island's biggest celebrity supporter. Even though he's super old, in his fifties now, he is a very, very handsome man, with salt-and-pepper hair and an irresistible smile. He is also the one who donated the land for this sanctuary.

Usually, Mr. Barky—another of his nicknames, along with

MB, and Hot Bod—comes to Dog Island once or twice a year, when he is free from his other movie star obligations. It's a really big deal. Generally that's when the newest robot dog model is unveiled.

Hot Bod gets photographed out and about with his new robot dog, the pictures are posted *everywhere*, and sales go through the roof. Or, as our founder Dorothy Blodgett likes to joke, "Through the woof." Mechanical Tail is part-owned by Marky Barky, so it's really a winning situation for everyone.

Everything gets a fresh coat of paint before he gets here. Dog Island is always beautiful, but when we're spruced up I feel especially proud.

"I guess so?" Wolf says.

"Me, too," I say. "Our house got painted. Bright pink." I shrug, as if I am trying to sort out some complicated feelings about having a newly pink house. My actual feelings about the house being very pink are: yay!

"Ours, too," says Wolf. "Green, though. I know yours is pink because I helped paint it."

"Oh yeah," I say.

This is torture. Why can't we just go back to the beach and make out some more? Every time we stop talking I start thinking about how he is so adorable, and I have dirt-brown eyes. Dirt on my skin, too. And a funny smell, I think. I try to discreetly sniff my armpit, and no, it is not good. *Oy*.

Billy yips and lifts his paw again to point. Another cat. A black one. There are still some old-timers out there—though not *here* per se—who get superstitious about black cats being unlucky. We know that really they are just hated because of myth and superstition. Which unfortunately turns into its own reality, driving people to do terrible things to these cats. Oh, the stories I've been told about these poor creatures being caught and tortured by horrible people; they've given me nightmares. It just all means black cats *especially* need our protection.

"Go get it, Billy," I say.

Billy dashes off and comes back with the cat. He drops it gently at my feet. I pick up the cat. It's black with a white chest and green eyes. Not electric looking. Organic eyes. Organic cat.

"You could get hurt out here," I say to the cat. I put it back down and pet its soft fur. The cat purrs and rubs against my ankles.

I unlock my phone so I can see the screen. I open the "Cat Report" app and hit a button, to let the Animal Safety Division know about this poor vulnerable being. They will come soon, to look for and capture the cat. They will make sure the cat never suffers.

"It smells nice out," Wolf says. "I love this time of year."

"Me, too," I say. I take a big whiff. Sweetness. Spring is in the air. It's a soapy smell. The "scent of renewal in nature," is how lofty old Dad puts it. ("It's the plants having sex and my allergies are terrible," is Mom's more usual take.)

And suddenly I remember that it smelled just like this last year, when Billy disappeared.

I stop tossing the ball to robot dog Billy. It can't really enjoy playing, anyway. It's a robot.

WOLF WALKS ME ALL the way home. When I'm walking with him these days, I can't help but *notice* all sorts of things that used to just be background.

To think, before Billy was gone, we were just old friends. Same as me and Jack. Same as him and Jack. The three of us were always together, from the time we were born. Our parents are all best friends, even. (Or were. They don't seem to hang out much anymore.)

But Jack stepped back after Billy went missing, just when Wolf came forward. Became essential. And now here we are. *Here we are.* I dance a couple of steps on the sidewalk and smile at Wolf. He seems so certain, of himself, of everything.

Our founder Dorothy Blodgett drives by in her custom GoPod. She honks and waves as she drives by. She must be going home to her Spanish-style house that overlooks the water.

Her GoPod is always so filthy—full of food wrappers and dirty paw protectors, and there's always something damp on the seat. She's funny for the leader of the world's most powerful animal movement. Messy and lovable. She's been married like six or seven times but says she's done with all *that* now. Now it's just about protecting animals.

We yell "Dog be with you" as loud as we can, and then laugh, and then kiss, and then walk.

"Dog be with *you*," Wolf says to me.

"No, with *you*, I must insist," I say back.

The Spanish moss dripping down over the oaks. The yards that are quickly becoming wild and unruly again after having been reduced to mostly dust and spiky cacti for so long. Mowing isn't allowed here at the sanctuary; mowing kills habitats for the birds and rodents and lizards. Those are still Organics, not robots, so they need to be protected to the utmost so they will not suffer.

There's that one palm tree that's grown so much taller than the others, a strong survivor of a tree. Then in my head I can hear Mom lecturing me: Palm trees aren't actually trees. They are grasses. If you cut them open, they don't have rings, like a tree. You couldn't tell how old they are by killing them. Mom says this every chance she gets, like it's extremely profound. Sometimes it seems profound. Sometimes it seems like the one fact she remembers from junior high school and won't quit mentioning.

So I say to Wolf: "Did you know that palm trees are grasses, not actually trees?"

"No, Nano," says Wolf. "You've never told me that before."

"It's true. If you cut them down—"

Wolf starts talking: "—they don't have any rings and you won't know how old they are. Killing them serves no purpose."

"So, ah, you've heard that one before."

"Only about forty million times," he says. "You can cut me down and see how many rings I have. That'll tell you exactly how many times you've told me this."

"Well maybe I will!" I shout.

"Please don't. Don't cut me down, little Nano," Wolf says.

"Okay, not yet," I say.

"Can we make out before we get you home?" Wolf asks.

"I think that would be okay," I say. I bite my lip. I smile.

My mouth is a little dry, but I don't care. The water we drink here is about 90 percent recycled pee that's been treated with chemicals. I had pure water once; my brother gave it to me—he said he "found" a bottle but I'm sure he probably stole it from somewhere. Ever since then I've always felt kind of dry mouthed and thirsty, no matter what. When it drizzles, those rare instances, I stand outside with my mouth open just to get another taste of the real thing.

Wolf and I step off the sidewalk and underneath one of the big old mostly dead trees about half a block from my house. My back is against the trunk. Once upon a time, you might get hurt when dead branches fell unexpectedly atop your head. But most of the branches with the potential to do serious harm fell a long time ago.

Wolf stands in front of me. He touches my face.

"Little Nano," he says, then leans in and kisses me. And kisses me. And kisses me.

Maybe an hour goes by. Maybe it's just thirty seconds.

"Nano, would you *please* get your behind home now, please," my mom orders, via Billy. Billy's tail is still wagging. It's humiliating. I am definitely letting Mechanical Tail know that I hate Billy's "human chat" function.

"You have nothing to wag about," I tell him.

"I do," says Wolf. He swishes his behind back and forth a couple of times. Then he asks me to turn around. I do, and he brushes sand out of my hair, off my shoulders.

"Now you're presentable," he says.

I give him one last peck on his cheek and run the last little bit to old 2644 28th Avenue, with its newly pink facade.

My parents really need to lose the pair of old pink plastic flamingos in the front "garden." It's nothing more than a rock-and-cactus collection, anyway.

Approaching, I catch a glimpse of a human-sized blur out of the corner of my eye. I'm probably just imagining things, I tell myself, trying to tamp down the sense of foreboding and doom that I've walked around with a lot, since Billy's disappearance.

Just imagining scary, terrible, frightening probably hopefully, hopefully, hopefully (I pray to Dog) not-true things. My robot dog would probably point if something were really there.

CHAPTER 2

Billy—human Billy—is my older brother. Was my older brother? I hope he is, still. He's ten years older than me. Or was, if he's dead, which I hope to Dog he's not.

Mom and Dad had Billy when they were teenagers, still living in Rhode Island. They had me in their late twenties. By then they were already on Dog Island—they were among the first people to move here, one of the "founding families" that moved to the sanctuary when the dog population got dangerously close to disappearing altogether. When Dog Island became the last hope.

Mom and Dad were busy saving dogs, saving the world, not to mention going to the beach, making friends, drinking fermented coconut juice, and so on. There was no school or daycare here, being as there were hardly any people at all, let alone kids. Just me and Billy, Jack and Wolf, and a couple of other kids whose families came for a year or two before deciding Dog Island wasn't for them.

So my brother played with me. He taught me things, like how to count and read. How to watch TV on his phone in our rooms without Mom and Dad noticing. That was back when we had more reliable Internet. He told me which leaves and fruits I could eat. Later I found out he mostly just made things up as we went along—it's lucky we didn't *die* eating pokeberries. Among other reasons: it would be humiliating to our mother if her own children were so ignorant about nature as to die from eating poisonous berries.

He and I and whatever robot dog we had at the time used to go out on these great long walks together, exploring every accessible inch of our two-square-mile hometown—the beaches, brick-paved streets, dozens of neon-colored old bungalow homes (about half-occupied, half-empty), a one-story motel where temporary volunteers and visitors shack up, largely abandoned old stores, a couple of parks, and no way to leave. No bridge to the mainland, no PlaneCabs at our disposal, no money to use even if you should leave; we are cashless and creditless here, just sharing what we have and getting what we need from the common pot. We knew everyone, they all knew us. It all seemed normal to me. I didn't—don't—know anything else.

On these walks, Billy would talk and talk and talk about everything. The part that fascinated me the most was when he'd tell me about being little in Rhode Island and the very different life he had there.

Billy was born in a small waterfront town called Wickford, which had been a colonial trading post but was now mostly for hippies and tourists and a small number of year-rounders. Mom and Dad had both grown up there, in houses next door to each other. When Mom got pregnant with Billy at age seventeen—whoopsie—she and Dad moved into a little apartment on top of Dad's parents' garage. And that's where they stayed for almost a decade.

Dad was a chef at a fish restaurant. Mom worked part-time as a kayak guide and went to the community college, then finished her bachelor's degree online. She got out with a joint degree in philosophy and wildlife biology and then kept working as a kayak guide. She liked the hours; she liked the scenery. She didn't so much like that her parents were always pressuring her to "go do something with yourself," is what I've been told.

This was right around the horrible experiment that led to the dogs becoming so dangerous and then so endangered. The experiment that led to their near demise and to our founder, Dorothy Blodgett, creating Dog Island, Dog bless her. So Billy and Mom and Dad had a family dog back then.

Billy told me about Dylan, who was a golden retriever, a real one, an Organic, a pet, who liked to play with a ratty tennis ball out in the yard. Dylan slept on Billy's bed, mushed up so close to Billy, he told me that sometimes he—Billy—would end up getting shoved all the way over to the edge and fall onto the floor. I couldn't even imagine what that would be like, being able to share a bed with a real dog. You might as well sleep with a tiger (if they hadn't gone extinct).

Billy told me about playing baseball with other kids. There not being a drought. What it was like to eat hamburgers ("wicked, wicked awesome" were his words for it). Not fauxburgers, but hamburgers, with slices of real melted cheese on top. I couldn't square what I knew about it being evil to keep sentient creatures like cows and pigs trapped in dark, painful circumstances for their whole lives before they die painful deaths and then become food, with Billy telling me about how much he enjoyed eating the hamburgers.

Back in his old life. Before Mom and Dad met Dorothy at a lecture at their local library, where she was talking about her newest book—*What We Owe Them: Goddamn Everything, An Animal Manifesto*—and were so inspired they decided to follow her to Florida, to Dog Island. Mom was six months pregnant with me at the time. That's how she got around the "no new human babies" Dog Island edict.

This pre–Dog Island life Billy told me about sounded so exotic and strange, idyllic and dark at the same time. I couldn't get enough of hearing about it. I only got to go to Wickford once, when Dad's parents died in a car wreck. Mom's mom was still alive at the time. She made me lunch, which Mom didn't let me eat even though I was hungry, and told me how "cute but boyish" I looked to her, then she cried, and I didn't know why, and she wouldn't say. I remember that the weather was cold, it was even cold inside Mom's house, and we didn't stay long enough for me to really see much beyond the funeral.

Of course things changed a little as we got older. I spent more time with Wolf and Jack and less time with my brother. Wolf and Jack and I had a lot to do on our own then, like going to the beach, kayaking, riding bikes, sitting around reading. We'd reenact scenes from our favorite TV shows and movies—which we could "stream" when our clunky Internet

was working, which was not very often, or, more often, we'd
get to see when someone trotted out an old television and
some tapes or DVDs for a Dog Island movie night down at the
beach or in the Casino. Like we all loved this stupid old show
called *The Bionic Woman,* and Jack and Wolf always wanted
me to play her in our reenactments. But I always wanted to
play her bionic dog, Max, instead.

I don't actually know what Billy was doing then. There
weren't really any other kids his age to play with. No permanent ones, anyway. Sometimes visitors would bring their
teenagers with them. Then he had a friend for a day or a
week or however long they were here. I know he had an
older girlfriend for a while and got an online degree in, like,
business management or something like that at some point.
Something Mom called "pedestrian but practical I suppose."

That was when the Internet was a little more reliable. He
always seemed to be just a little bit adrift, always looking for
something. He listened to a lot of music in his room, and
there was a smell that followed him around—a smell I rec-
ognized with acute precision the first time Jack lit up some
weed in front of me.

Then, maybe five years ago, Billy got recruited to be part
of Dog Island's We Are Guardians unit, otherwise known as
WAG. That's the group that was formed to investigate and
stop animal cruelty across the country. Dorothy got every gov-
ernor in the country to grant her the authority to dispatch
WAG into their states, when needed. To do our best to make
sure that no other animals would suffer, like the dogs had.

Billy spent most of his time, after that, traveling around

the country, investigating animal abuse allegations—then that evidence could be brought to prosecutors.

When Billy first started with We Are Guardians, WAG, he'd come back home with horrific, nightmarish tales of the things he'd seen. A family that moved out of its cockroach-filled apartment but left two cats—a mom and baby—behind. The mom had eaten most of her baby's body before being discovered. There was a friendly pet pig set on fire by some drunk teenagers who kept screaming about how much they loved bacon. A horse bashed in the head with a golf club by the owner's boyfriend when she threatened to leave him for another man.

These stories inspired Billy's work, as much as they sickened me. He stopped talking about wanting to eat hamburgers; when he was home that distinctive smell didn't emanate from his room as often. Also when he was home, he'd say he just couldn't wait to get back out on the road again, to "bring justice to the voiceless."

After a few years of this, though, something seemed to change again. We'd still go for walks together when he was around. But he stopped telling me stories about his investigations, about his heinous investigations. I'd ask him about them, and he'd give me a look that seemed both stricken and numb. He'd just say, "It can't keep going like this."

"What can't?" I'd ask. He'd shake his head, change the subject.

I really miss him, now. One day Billy was here. I remember he was fighting with Dad about something. Mom was crying. They sent me over to Jack's for dinner. When I got back that night Billy was still at home. But he wouldn't talk to me, just stayed in his room listening to music. By the time I woke up the next day, he was gone. All his device trackers disabled.

Mom and Dad told me they didn't know where he'd gone or why. They said the police were on it; they said we should pray to Dog that Billy would be back, safe, before too long. That was a year ago now. Best I know, there've been no leads. We have no Billy. I'm not sure what we do have, without him.

BILLY, MY ROBOT DOG, and I go inside.

"I'm home!" I call out.

"Oh honey, good," I hear Mom yell from the kitchen. "Come in and help me set the table."

Billy and I walk through our dusty, musty, cheerful living room and into the tiled kitchen, where Mom is looking sweaty and happy stirring something over the stove. The robot vacuum cleaner is whirring around the room, cleaning up after her. It's very cute; they made it to look like a little elephant that sucks up dirt with its trunk. This is as close as we really have to elephants anymore, since the real ones went extinct, since they were mostly hunted out of existence, and the few ones left died of starvation, their food and water gone from the drought. I never even got to see one in person, before they were gone.

"I tried a new stew," Mom tells me. "It's got acorns in it. I thought it might help with my allergies."

"Isn't it a little hot out for that?" I ask.

"Yes," Mom says. "As it turns out yes, it is a little hot out for that. But it's made. Can you get out bowls and plates? Dad is out back grilling. Is Wolf coming for dinner?"

"Yes," I say. "Yes to setting the table. No to Wolf."

"Okay!" Mom says. "How about Jack?"

"No to Jack, too," I say.

"I miss those boys. They used to be here every night," Mom says. "Times change, I guess. How do you kids keep getting older while Dad and I stay our same youthful selves?"

"It's a real mystery," I say, standing on my toes to collect bowls and plates from the second shelf in the cabinets. (Mom is tall, like Billy. I am not, like Dad.)

I carry them outside. Dad is at the grill. It smells good, which sadly does not necessarily correspond to the food tasting good.

"What are you making?" I ask.

"Ethical Chicken patties," Dad says. "I thought I'd make you into my guinea pig. Word on the street is they do *not* taste like vomit."

My dad being the chef of the Dog Island community cafeteria, we're always getting samples and handouts as the lab-grown meat market expands.

Many of the samples are, as Billy used to put it, "wicked wretched." It tastes okay to me. I've only ever eaten this. It's not like I am out there missing something else.

"What does this one look like?" I ask Dad.

"Don't ask," he says. "But it smells good, right, kitten?"

"Fantastic," I say, placing the plates and bowls around our glass-topped table.

"It smells a lot like what real chicken used to smell like

on the grill," Dad says to me now. Apparently chicken is the topic that gets him going these days.

"I can't tell if that's a good thing or a bad thing. I've spent a lot of my later life avoiding eating things that smell like this," he continues. I love when he tells me stories about his old life. I wish he'd do it more. He and Billy were closer than he and I are. They talked more, and fought more.

"It smells good to me," I say. Billy's nose is up in the air, sniffing. He looks quite pleased. "I think Billy likes it, too."

"Huh," Dad replies. I press the "positive interaction" button because it's cute to see a robot dog seeming to enjoy the smell of food, and also it's pleasant to see Dad engaging a little, too. He retreats to the Parents' Room a lot more now than before, claiming he's swamped with work. As the Dog Island chef, it's hard to see what work he might be doing in that room, but perhaps he's just experimenting with low-water cocktail recipes.

The food's done cooking. Dad puts the "chicken" onto fresh-made buns he picked up from Dog Island Sourdough Vegan Bakers earlier in the day, and Mom ladles out the hot stew and cool salad.

Mom and Dad drink glasses of fermented coconut wine that their friends Owen and Bob make in a big vat in their backyard and then distribute to all the boozy adults in this community. Mom claims that it helps with her allergies. Dad claims he likes being tipsy. They do not allow me to partake, which seems mean, and silly. I know where they hide their stuff.

I bite into the sandwich and immediately regret it. This food is appalling.

"Well, I don't think I will be serving this twice," Dad says.

Mom nods. "It's repellent. Want more salad?"

"Sure," I say. She uses the tongs to put some greens and other veggies on my plate. It's good to have real, grown veggies again. Not to have to eat so much stupid cactus.

"Billy would have hated this salad," I say. "Remember how he used to say that the only good thing about the drought was not having to eat so many vegetables?"

Mom chuckles then reaches over and rubs my arm. "He really hated vegetables," she agrees.

"Hated?" I say. My heart speeds up. "Hated?"

"Come on, kittencakes," Mom says, quietly. Dad looks down. It's not such a change for Dad to eat without really saying much, but Mom doesn't stop talking in exclamation points very often. She's "ebullient" is how I've heard her described. "Loudmouth," is another description that some cattier members of the community—the Bad Bitches—have used. She puts the trait to good use as the spokesperson for Dog Island. She can, as she says, "spokes and spokes and spokes some more" when she feels like it.

"Don't you wonder where he is?" I ask them. I try not to ask it too often. It bothers them, to be asked, and I don't like to be a bother. I just wish that he was with us. And that, if he wasn't, then we could at least share the sadness and confusion about him being gone. It must hurt them as much as it hurts me. He's their kid.

"Of course," Mom says. "Of course. We miss him like crazy. Dad and I both do. It seems like just yesterday he was coming out of my body. Such a perfect tiny baby. Oh, how I loved being pregnant with him, giving birth. And of course with you, too."

"Of course. Shouldn't we be out looking for him, then?"

"Oh, Nano-baby," Mom says. "Hey, I have an idea! Want to come with me to feed the dogs tonight?"

I feel two conflicting emotions: Confused, about why we can't talk about my brother being missing, possibly dead. And thrilled, doggone thrilled, at the prospect of getting to see the dogs. Despite spending my whole life on Dog Island, I rarely get to spend any time with the dogs themselves. This is mostly because of them being very vicious and dangerous, so they don't get much human contact to start off with. It's especially rare for one of the kids to get to go into their enclosure. Which we call the "Ruffuge," on account of really liking dog puns here.

Which means I'm excited as all get-out as I scrape the leftover Ethical Chicken sandwiches into our compost bin and load up the plates and bowls into the Dish Blower; then I go into my room to get my dog suit—the formfitting garment that we all wear when going to visit the dogs. It emits special pheromones to mask our human scent (and less importantly, our appearance) so that the dogs won't attack us.

It's been ages since Mom let me come with her to help feed the dogs and make sure they are all safe and accounted for. I hope I can find my suit. I hope it still fits.

I rifle through my closet—some pants, tops, shorts, and dresses, mostly made out of that stiff perma-clean cloth that can be "washed" every once in a while with some air blowing, or, when really dirty, a laser. No dog suit. Crap, where is it? No suit, no dogs.

I yank a big cardboard box out from the closet. It's where I throw the things that I don't have any current use for, but also don't want to get rid of. I can't imagine why it'd be in the box, but I also can't think of where else it'd be. I start pulling out T-shirts that are too small, a broken radio that I might fix one day, an ear belonging to Snowflake, one of my first robot dogs—back then, they used to just spontaneously fall apart a lot more. An ear might fall off, or a tail. Big patches of fur might disintegrate if the robot dog was caught in some rain. I smile, remembering Snowflake. She was really a complete wreck by the time Mechanical Tail came to terminate her, to replace her with . . . How can I forget who came after Snowflake? It was either Bruno or Ninja . . .

But still no sign of the dog suit.

I approach the closet again, *willing* this dog suit to be there, taking out one garment at a time to try to track this thing down. Finally, when the small closet is totally empty, I see a little ball of silky faux fur at the back of the closet. A mask, with long floppy ears, is buried under the suit. Thank *Dog*. I nearly cry with gratitude.

"Nano? Darling?"

I ignore Mom and slip the suit on over my clothes, worried it will be too small, given that it's been a very long time since I last wore it. Instead, oddly, it's too big. I haven't gotten smaller myself, so I can't think of why this would be, but there's really no time to think about this particular puzzle right now. Instead I race into the front room, almost tripping over the extra fabric and hoping Mom doesn't notice.

Mom has on her dog suit. It is quite formfitting. She holds her mask in one hand and wiggles her butt in a way that would be embarrassing if it were in public, but she'd do it anyway. "We've got to get a shake on, sweetheart!"

"I'm ready," I say, holding my mask.

Mom and I say goodbye to Dad, who gives me a strangely long hug and kisses the top of my head, and get into a GoPod parked on the street—the self-driving golf cart–sized, solar-powered vehicles that people use to get around the parts of our sanctuary where there are roads or paths. Except for Dorothy's, they aren't owned, they belong to the community; anyone who has been registered can use them.

Mom presses her thumb into the ignition button and puts the top down. It's such a beautiful night. There's a great big red moon in the sky and we are going to see the dogs. As we ride along, Mom rubs my fur-covered arm with one of her hands, which is covered in her dog suit so looks like a paw. I can't sit still, I'm so excited.

It's about a mile to the entrance of the Ruffuge. To get there we rumble in our GoPod through more residential streets, paved in brick, and lined with little brightly colored bungalows like the one that we live in.

We drive along the beach for a while, the big red moon hovering over the horizon, then turn onto a dark unpaved road. It smells like dirt and jungle and flowers and salt water—so feral, so delicious.

After a couple of minutes, we approach the only gate onto

the Ruffuge itself, which is about twenty-five acres, jutting out on a little peninsula surrounded by water. This one spot is the only land-based point of access.

Mom gets out of the GoPod to check in with the night security guard, then comes back out carrying a huge box, with tonight's rations in it.

"George wants to say shalom," she says. "Go on in."

I walk into the guard's room hanging onto the fabric of my dog suit to try to keep the pants from dragging on the ground. George is sitting at his console in front of 25 or so screens, all showing different parts of Dog Island. I don't know how he stays focused on these screens for so many hours at a time. I'd end up reading a book, falling asleep, going out for a wander, playing ball with my robot dog, shooting the poop with my buddies, and so on. Guess it's a good thing George is doing this job and not me.

"Nano!" George calls out, turning away from the screens. "It's so wonderful to see you."

"Shalom, George," I say, kissing his scratchily bearded cheek. George is one of the old-timers. He wears his long gray hair in a ponytail, matched by a long beard that is, for some reason, still brown. He always looks like he's a little stoned, and almost never wears shoes. Like almost everyone who lives here, his arms and legs are covered in tattoos. Lots of paw prints and animal faces, among other things. (My dorky parents are two of the only grown-ups who aren't inked all over; they sport a pair of mortifyingly corny matching tats they got in their teens: a single rose, on their ankles.)

"Anything good to see tonight?" I ask, gesturing at the monitors.

"Yep. Just like every night," George says. We watch the monitors together for a couple of minutes. We can see the dogs sitting still, near where we will be feeding them soon. You could tell the time by these animals. Seeing them, still, always, makes my heart stop for a second. They are all different shapes and sizes, and they are all magnificent. Both cute and terrifying, important and goofy. At once, you can have a sort of religious feeling toward them—the thank *Dogs* are partly to be funny and partly dead-serious—but then you just have to see these beasties playing with a new toy, or wrestling with each other, to see how *delightful* they are as well. How earthly. How Organic. These animals embody the best of everything.

Now they're howling and yipping. "Well, you'd better get going. The dogs are getting hungry," George says.

I give George an awkward hug and then head back into the GoPod. The first gate opens. We drive into the holding section, where we'll stay until the first gate closes. Then the second gate will open. My heart's pounding. I'm going to get to see the *dogs*.

Mom puts on her mask and indicates for me to do the same. We can't let the dogs smell our breath or our human scent. The mask is too big, too, but just a little. If it doesn't stay on, I could be killed. If I take it off and tell Mom what's happening, who knows when I can come back here.

So I wear it and hope. Mom puts the GoPod's top up and switches the vehicle over to manual. The drivable paths inside the Ruffuge are constantly being remade and our AutoDrive function won't work here.

We inch forward. The GoPod's headlights are set to "night vision." There's an eerie, spectral glow. We can see the dense expanse of trees and plants—the types that grow hardily, even with the drought. Some palms and other leafy plants but mostly spiny ones, like cacti, pretty and sharp.

You can hear the waves crashing on the beach and the birds making their nighttime songs. They sound like beautiful ghosts. I look up into the sky, where the stars are so bright, the red moon huge and luminous.

Mom is a nervous driver. She's better in a kayak. She inches the GoPod along the dark path. I'm staring out the window. I know it's unlikely we'll see any dogs until our food drop-off, but a girl can dream.

After what feels like hours, we stop. Mom gets out of the GoPod. I follow. There's a chance she'll tell me to get back inside the cart since this part of the mission is where we'd get killed, if we were going to get killed. But she doesn't tell me to come back into the cart.

The dogs are here. Five magnificent dogs, who watch us intently as I help Mom unload the container of rations from the GoPod trunk. As she unpacks, the dogs begin making their soft grunts to tell us they are excited and impatient, and my heart pounds to be near them.

There are six portions of food, each given out in an edible container. I watch as Mom walks before each of the incredible dogs—not named, just numbered, since we are not to ever forget they are wild—and places a container in front of it.

They look at her for a second—a long second, during which anything could happen, and nothing does—and then they tear into their food. The edible containers are designed to take a little while to get into, to give the humans time to look the dogs over while they're distracted—to ensure nothing is wrong that requires attention.

Something is wrong, though. One of the dogs is missing.

"Where is she?" Mom mutters, looking around and rubbing her temples, which in other circumstances would look kind of funny given that she's wearing a dog mask and rubbing them with her paws. Like a dog is saying, "Oy vey!" But right now it's just pretty serious.

Mom whistles. She shakes the remaining container. We wait.

"How do you feel about going for a little hike?" Mom asks me brightly.

Mom and I activate the low-glow lights that are embedded in our dog masks. Then she walks off one way, and I walk up a hill, to the tallest point in the Ruffuge, where I think I hear a little rustling. I'm off the trail, in the thick of the jungle, trying to stay calm as I walk toward the noise.

Following the sound, I crouch on the ground and check underneath a bush. Pushing aside the thorny branches, I see that there, indeed, is the missing dog. She's a red-furred beauty with a wide flat face, lying in a patch of dirt. With four beautiful itty-bitty black-and-white puppies beside her.

They look at me, big-eyed, scared, curious. Three bare their teeth while hiding under their mother.

One does something miraculous and impossible: begins to wag its tiny tail.

Mechanical Tail now offers three models of robot dogs!
Each is fully customizable in terms of color and size.

Are you looking for a lovable LUNK who will happily
sit with you on the couch? Meet FIDO! How about an
active robot dog who will stick by your side through a
marathon? That's CORKIE!

And if it's home security that's your game, get to know
THEODORE! No thieves will get past this big boy!
GRRR!!

Come meet ALL our robot dog models at any of our
showrooms, or call 1-800-ROBOTDG to arrange a visit
from one of our exciting MOBILE showrooms.

CHAPTER 3

I've spent my whole life on Dog Island, and so I tend to assume everyone knows its history like I do; that everyone grew up hearing about the tragic human folly that led to Dog Island becoming necessary.

That everyone would know inside and out why seeing this puppy wag its tail would so affect me.

Just in case you don't, here's the terrible long and short of it.

About twenty-five years ago, some scientists thought it would be a smart idea to try and tinker with some dogs' genes. They thought making a couple of little tweaks to the DNA would make these dogs and their progeny even more useful than they already were.

Now mind you, these dogs were already extremely useful—like Wooly, one of the most famous canines, who was the service dog for a New Yorker named Maya who was blind and deaf and also suffered a life-threatening heart condition.

Because of Wooly, Maya could have a real life. She walked and rode subways safely. He also helped her get dressed, put away the dishes and laundry, and ordered refills of her prescriptions using a special app developed for this purpose. He turned the lights in their apartment on and off and knew what button to press for an ambulance should Maya need that kind of help. Oh yeah, Wooly was also trained to know when Maya *needed* an ambulance.

Wooly was so incredible that he became the subject of a documentary. That documentary inspired dog trainers to try and teach dogs to do even *more*. Cook a simple meal, fly an airplane, deliver the mail, do some basic computer coding, and so on. There was no reason for dogs to *have* to do these things. Fairly complex tasks that could be automated were mostly being handled by robots by that point, with the technology getting better every day. Then some scientists got excited about what might happen if they made a few tweaks here and there to the dogs' DNA. Obviously that subjected a whole lot of dogs to a whole lot of painful, unnecessary laboratory testing. Which was just one of what turned out to be a lot of really, really awful things associated with these experiments.

But these scientists! No stopping them once they've got an idea they want to pursue.

They mucked around with the dogs' DNA. They messed up. The dogs they experimented on were still not able to fly airplanes. Instead, these dogs just got angry and upset and vicious, and lost the qualities that had made dogs our best companions for the preceding 50,000 years. They stopped wanting to be with us, they stopped doing the things that we loved so much—wagging their tails, licking us affectionately, sleeping with us at night. Now, instead, they wanted to kill us.

That seemed to be the main effect of the experiments: creating a laboratory full of dogs who really hated humans. If there is any comfort to be found in this misguided project, it's that at least the horrible scientists got bitten a lot. Which would be funnier if it hadn't led to where we are now.

Because somehow the changed DNA spread. It is said to have "migrated" from the unlucky lab dogs to *all* dogs, like a virus. How exactly did that happen? I don't have the answer to that question. I'm seventeen, not a scientist myself, and the only school I ever really got was on the Internet, and like I told you our Internet doesn't work very well. I recommend you go look it up if you want more information about the technical side of this disaster.

I can tell you that the last generation of "pets" died out within about a decade. People kept buying and adopting and breeding new dogs. But they couldn't live with them in ways that were safe for the humans or for the dogs. It got really, really ugly.

Because the situation was so unsafe, the dogs obviously couldn't be kept as they'd been. They didn't live inside with their families anymore; they didn't sleep in their beds. The people who still held onto their dogs—out of duty, or love, or for any other reason—mostly kept these animals chained up outside or locked in basements. The dogs got food and water thrown at them, if they got fed and watered at all. Many starved to death, only being unchained or unlocked once they were dead, and therefore no longer dangerous.

Other dogs were set free. Gangs of them would terrorize neighborhoods. Attack old people and children especially—the weakest and most vulnerable among us. The dogs would be shot and beaten, intentionally hit by cars. People left out bowls of poisoned food, which led to slow and painful deaths for dogs and any other animals or people that happened to take a bite. It was grotesque and awful for everyone.

Dorothy Blodgett, our founder, had been working as an immigration lawyer, when all this began. She specialized in securing refugee status for people fleeing politically unstable countries. Given the fraught times and the urgency created by the water wars, she was very busy and very successful.

Dorothy was so horrified by the violence, the death, the suffering, that she put aside her legal work and set about trying to help restore peace for people and for dogs.

First, Dorothy opened a massive sanctuary in Texas, where her family had a big ranch. She created expansive, comfortable enclosures for the dogs, so they would be safe and happy. But there were problems. For one, it was extremely difficult to collect all the dogs, given their number, and how ferocious they were. Then there was the issue of transporting the dogs to Texas. This would be hard enough if we were just dealing with dogs from the United States. But the bum genetic changes had traveled the world.

It's not like things were great even for the dogs who got to Texas—which they did, by the thousands. They were miserable at the ranch. The dogs hated being enclosed. You could hear it in their mournful howls; in the way they hurt themselves, seemingly on purpose, flinging their bodies at the gates that prevented their freedom. Their bones broke, and so did Dorothy's spirit.

Dorothy wept as she watched what became of the creatures she'd promised to protect and care for. She wept thinking about the dogs who were still loose, still imperiled, about the suffering she felt helpless to end. Plus she got terrible press as a few journalists came to the ranch and saw the dogs' unhappiness, their empty water bowls. This caused public opinion to turn against her plan, which previously had attracted great support.

Dorothy found herself facing what she considered the only humane solution. It was a terrible solution, she felt, but unavoidable: she would have to kill the dogs to save them, and she would have to convince the public and lawmakers to let her do it and moreover to enforce that mandate by disallowing private citizens from owning or keeping dogs.

Dorothy shared this awful conclusion with a small, trusted inner circle. One of them was a biochemist. The biochemist helped Dorothy develop a compound still used today to end the dogs' suffering. It's called Kinderend and is administered with a spritz on or in the nose; it is painless and near-instant.

Another of Dorothy's closest companions then was a young aspiring actor. It's rumored he was also Dorothy's lover. I wish the people who spread that rumor would use a word other than "lover," which feels old and just plain creepy. Back then, this aspiring actor was called Marcus Muhlenberg. Now, of course, he's Marky Barky. (I hear the Bad Bitches describe him as having "a very sexy physique." I would not personally use those exact words because I am not ancient.)

Marky Barky told Dorothy about Beachport. He'd grown up in nearby Tampa and knew that the town had basically been abandoned once the weather patterns changed too much to make a former Florida fishing village much of a current vacation destination. Beachport used to be connected with the mainland, but due to the ocean levels rising, it had become an island. There was no bridge or anything; the only way there was—is—by boat or aircraft. It was still habitable though, he told her. And would make a great place to start fresh with a new sanctuary for any dogs that could be saved.

At first Dorothy rejected the idea. It was too arbitrary to save some dogs but not the rest. And for what? We tried to keep them alive, and all it did was make them suffer. We did this to them, she said. We owe it to them to give them peace.

Even then, Marky Barky knew how to read an audience. He correctly grasped that Dorothy's plan to gather a small army who would travel the world administering her peace-granting nose spray with the government's backing, was medicine that wouldn't go down so easily—unless there was a little sugar on top. The sugar was Dog Island.

Marky Barky was right. Dog Island was an instant hit. People from all over donated tons of money—millions upon millions of dollars. Enough to put this place together and support its inhabitants. There was even enough left that Marky Barky and his business partner could pour some cash into Mechanical Tail—get that outfit kicking and build a business that could support our mission here financially and otherwise.

The thing is that even with all that money, all those resources, the Ruffuge here is only able to house six dogs at a time. We just don't have space for more than that. More than that, they fight; they are miserable. More than that, they *suffer*. So there is a strict birth control regimen—hormones in their food to carefully maintain reproduction.

But the birth control isn't fully effective. So every once in a while, there's an unexpected litter. And then, that's where we are now.

I call out: "Mom! Mom, over here."

Her footsteps are heavy as she walks to me.

"You found the dog?"

"Yeah. But that's not all," I say.

Mom, in her dog mask, looks at me. I can't see her real face, but I'm imagining the expression. She always looks so open and friendly, cheerful toward the world. My face, behind my mask, is anguished.

"There are puppies," I tell her. "Three of them."

"Three?" she asks.

It's not too late. I could say, "Oh no, sorry, there's four."

I think of the puppy's tiny tail, swishing back and forth. Like a robot dog's does. But *real*.

"Three," I say. "I saw three."

Mom asks me to get the puppies and bring them to her. I do, one by one. Mom chants a mantra, a blessing, to each as she administers the spray: "Be pacified. Be loved. I bring you peace and happiness. Let's proceed."

The spritz of Kinderend. The end. Peace. Their tiny bodies are placed in a woven satchel in the GoPod's trunk. They will be cremated at the Dog Island Chapel.

There's something different for the mother dog. She has a medicated treat. It is formulated to dry up any remaining milk and give her euphoria for twenty-four hours, so she won't grieve her stolen puppies. I toss the treat her way, watch her sniff it, eat it. I think about the fourth puppy. What will happen to this one, with its siblings gone, with its mother euphoric? Its tail wagging?

"Ready, kitten?" Mom asks me.

"Yeah," I say.

Mom and I walk through the jungle back to the GoPod. The dogs will have finished their meals, so who knows where they are now. Hopefully, the dog suits will protect us.

They do. We don't even see the dogs again before getting back in the GoPod. We drive back along the path, back out the Ruffuge gate. Mom stops in to talk to George, telling him about the puppies.

"We need better surveillance cameras," she says, when she returns. She puts the GoPod into AutoDrive. "Dammit. George missed those puppies so long. They shouldn't have gotten that big. We should have known about them a week ago, at least. We probably also need better Georges. Jesus. This shouldn't have happened. Dorothy will not be happy."

She seems really agitated.

"What would be wrong if we just left them?" I ask.

"Left them?"

"The puppies. If we didn't . . . you know. If they grew up."

Mom doesn't answer right away. She takes off her dog mask, shakes out her hair. Her face is all sweaty.

"Honey," she finally says. "Kitten. It is our job to make sure that nothing bad ever happens to these dogs. It's the whole reason why we are here. Letting these puppies live sounds nice, right? But then there is overcrowding in the Ruffuge. Under these conditions, the dogs attack one another. They could get hurt and suffer. And even worse than that, what if they kill one another? What if the last dogs on earth die on our watch? It sounds so easy. Let some puppies live. It's not so easy. It's a system that requires strict adherence to rules in order to work. If we don't follow those rules, the whole system blows up. We lose our home. The dogs die. Everything . . ." Mom makes the universal sign for "explosion" with her fingers.

"But they're so little," I say.

"This way they never suffer," Mom says. "There are fates worse than death." It's the line that everyone uses here whenever the topic of euthanasia comes up. Which it does, sometimes—a visitor will bring it up, a journalist. Me. There are fates worse than death.

"What if there are fates that are better?" I ask Mom. "What if those puppies could have had rich, fulfilling lives? Good lives."

I'm thinking of the puppy I left behind now. Worried about that puppy. Hopeful for that puppy. Should I say something to Mom?

"Oh, honey. We tried that. It didn't work. Our species can't be trusted. These innocent animals, beings, would have suffered. That would have been their fate. Along with all the other dogs as well," Mom says. "And us, too, because that would mean the end of Dog Island, so our home would be gone." She smiles at me, says, "It's good to question the dogma sometimes, Nano. Be careful who you do it with. You're safe with me, of course."

Mom and I take the GoPod to the Dog Island Chapel on the other side of Dog Island. It takes maybe twenty minutes to get there. I love the chapel. A former Dog Islander named Mark built it before he died of cancer, maybe twenty years ago. Before I was born. The chapel is small and made of wood. There are only four pews, and each is carved to look like a dog. So we call them the "paws." The altar at the front is in the shape of a bone.

Mark made all this as tribute to his own dog, Snoopy, whose loss he grieved deeply. Not only because Snoopy, his companion, was gone, but because she'd be his last dog. She died right when that mutated gene was discovered to have spread almost completely. She was among the last unaffected generation.

The whole chapel is covered in notes that visitors have written, then thumbtacked to the walls. In the old days, the notes were about pets who'd died. You're not supposed to read them, but there isn't always a lot to do, so Wolf, Jack, and I have gone through a bunch. They say things like, *Barky, you are the best friend I ever had and I'll never forget you. RIP good girl. We'll play ball again in Heaven, Dog willing.*

Over the years, we get fewer notes like those because fewer people have even experienced a pet dog. Now they are a little more abstract, but just as heartfelt. More like, *Dogs, I am sorry for what we've done to you. Please, please, forgive us.*

There's a furnace out back, away from this part of the

chapel. Mom and I step out of our dog suits, which are flammable, and she places each puppy's soft, black-and-white body in a wooden box. Each is then placed inside the furnace. Mom chants a different mantra while doing it: "You are one with the universe. You have peace. You are loved."

I can't stop thinking about the fourth puppy. That puppy's body going into the furnace. I try to think about this correctly: no suffering. I just can't. I can't. My mind won't go that way this time. That puppy's tail, it *wagged*.

Mom and I go back home. She says she's going right to bed, then reminds me I should also get a good night's sleep since we have "a very busy day tomorrow because of Marky Barky, and do you think he'll like my haircut?"

"Of course he will," I say. But on the other hand maybe not. Women on Dog Island used to have one of three hairdos: uncut hair to the butt, a buzz cut, or a choppy bob with bangs. (I've had all three. Right now, I've got the choppy bob.)

Maybe two years ago, a former hairdresser named Bonnie moved over after getting a divorce back on the mainland. So now, in addition to those styles, we have several "glamour girl" options. Mom got one of these last time she went to see Bonnie. It looks sort of stiff and silly to me and requires hair spray to stay in place. Perhaps that's Marky Barky's thing, for all I know.

Mom kisses the top of my head before she goes into her and Dad's room. I can hear him snoring from the Parents' Room down the hall. He sometimes "rests his poor old eyes" in that room on the cup holder couch, if he and his robot bartender have spent a lot of time together.

"I love you, you know," she says to me.

I hug her. "I love you, too," I say back.

She pauses. "Do you know why I call you my kitten?"

"Because you love me?" I respond.

"That, too," Mom says. She sounds exhausted. "It's what my mom called me. I have no idea where she came up with the nickname, though. She was afraid of cats. I wish you'd really known my mother. Maybe it's the nickname you'll use for your own daughter one day."

"I guess I might not have kids ever," I say. It's actually never even occurred to me that I *might*.

"Then I guess you'll be the last kitten," Mom says. "There are fates worse than being the last kitten." She comes to me and kisses my forehead, then retreats to her bedroom.

I wander into the living room. Plop down on the non-cup holder couch. My robot dog Billy comes meandering out of my room and hops up beside me. He's giving me some serious eyes, then kind of leans into me and lifts a leg, to show me his belly. I rub it. His hind leg shakes. I think of the puppy, alone, in the jungle. If the puppy survives the night, which is a big if, then he or she will surely be discovered early tomorrow, when the morning shift comes to feed the dogs. That'll be the end, then.

Pulling my phone out, I send a PrivateText to Wolf and Jack: You guys awake?

CHAPTER 4

I sneak out of the house ever so quietly, carrying the dog suit in a tote bag, telling Billy my robot dog to stay put, even though he gives me a sad, hurt look. I grab my bike from the garage and head over to meet Wolf and Jack in our usual spot near the beach.

They're both there with their dog suits, as I instructed, carrying their masks. Jack, also as I instructed, is without Mr. Chi-Chi Pants just this once. He is smoking some weed. (I did not tell him to do that, but it's not shocking.) Wolf is tapping his foot and looking dreamy.

"What's up?" Wolf asks me.

"I need your help," I say. "But it's dangerous."

"Danger is my middle name," says Wolf.

"No it's not. John is your middle name," says Jack. The two of them start to scuffle, as they often do, shoving and punching. It looks pretty funny when they are in their dog suits. But not now.

"C'mon guys," I say. I explain what we will need to do.

Wolf looks a little wide-eyed, when I give him the details. Keeps saying, "Yeah, cool, okay, cool. I can help."

Jack just says, "Are you sure?"

I say, "Yes, I am." *Sure* isn't even the right word. I feel as if this is necessary. Not a choice. Compelled, impelled, I cannot do anything else.

We ride our bikes to the Ruffuge's security gate. I go inside the booth. George is still sitting there, still watching the monitors.

"Hiya again!" I say, kissing his cheek.

"Nano," George says, in his slow voice. "Shalom. What a treat, seeing you twice in one day."

"You, too," I reply. "Hey, so, my mom forgot something when we were in there tonight. She asked me to come back and get it for her. Wolf and Jack are here, too, so we can look out for each other."

"What did she forget?" George asks.

"Uh—her ID," I say.

"You think you'll be able to find that little thing at night like this?" George says.

"She really wants it tonight," I say.

"Let me give Ruby a call, Nano. I just can't see your mother sending her only daughter in there at night for an ID badge, even with two strapping young lads accompanying you. This can definitely wait until daylight. I'll just have the morning shift pick it up when they go in. Let's see if Uncle George here can't clear this up," he says, in a voice I know he means to be reassuring, while pulling out his phone.

"Call Ruby Miller," George is commanding his phone, when I interrupt.

"No, no; you're right, George," I say. "I'll go home and tell Mom that it's *crazy* to do this tonight. She can wait. It's not like anyone doesn't know who she is here. What does she even need ID for?"

"There you go," George says.

I walk back outside shaking my head. "No-go," I say, furrowing my brow.

"You want to just go hang out at the beach?" Wolf asks, which gives me an idea.

"You're brilliant," I tell him.

"He is?" Jack says.

Wolf takes my hand and smooches me hard on the mouth. "I am," he says.

We get our bikes and ride the 15 minutes or so over to the beach. Jack goes to sit down on the sand, but I tell him and Wolf we're not stopping yet. I have another idea: kayaks. There's a pile of them by the dock, for Dog Islanders' use. It's not impossible . . .

"Kayaks?" Jack asks skeptically.

"Yes," I say, with more confidence than I feel.

We trod to the kayaks, grab some paddles. Jack and Wolf will be in a double boat, I've got the single and lead the way. The moon is huge above us. The birds are making their soft nighttime sounds. As we paddle, a manatee swims up beside, pokes its soft nose out of the water, with spiky little hairs around the muzzle. This could be another relaxing evening out in this perfect place.

"Hi, manatee," I say, before it swims away. I have always had this feeling of communion with all animals, like the manatee knows I'm its friend—the cats, the birds, the fishes, too. Hopefully, also the dogs. We can hear their howls.

We paddle and paddle and finally reach the outer edge of the Ruffuge, thick with mangroves. I pull myself as close to shore as I can. Balancing carefully so I don't end up falling into the water—it's shallow here, but the bottom is sharp with oyster shells, and the water is cold—I tie my kayak up to a branch.

Jack, who is at the front of the double kayak, moves to do the same. He falls into the water and causes a loud splash. "Crap!" he yells.

"Be quiet," I say sharply, knowing that if anything goes wrong everything goes wrong.

"Sorry," Jack says, sounding genuinely chagrined.

On the thin strip of beach, I look at the fence enclosing the Ruffuge, try to convince myself I can climb it. It's only six feet. Maybe seven. Just a little barbed wire up top. Sure, why not, why not? I think. It's not like anything is electrified. Probably?

I grab the fence to start climbing, and—

Wrong. A jolt, sudden pain everywhere, brain scrambling, it hurls me into the air. I'm not sure if I black out. There are stars and then there are actual stars in the sky. I am lying on my back. I blink once, twice. I hear Wolf's voice beside me.

"Nano, are you okay?"

I move my fingers, toes, arms. I sit up. Everything tingles. The pain fades, not as fast as I'd like. I'm shaking. Okay. So, the fence is electrified.

"The trick is to jump onto the fence," says Jack. "You can't close the circuit by touching the ground while you touch the fence."

I stare at the fence, warily. What the hell? The first shock didn't kill me, anyway. I throw myself at it, leaping up a foot and holding on as high as I can. No shock. No shock! Big shock, that no shock.

I scramble up and carefully navigate over the barbed wire up top, only just grazing the crotch of my dog suit a little bit, but no rip, no tear.

Once I'm over, Wolf does the same. Jack just watches us. He's more bookish than Wolf is. He puts on his mask and then flings himself at the fence, just right. But he has a hard time pulling himself up, to climb to the top. He falls. Tries again. Shocks himself. Falls hard.

"You guys go," Jack finally says, still sitting on the ground, breathing heavily. "I'll make sure no one steals the kayaks."

With the low-glow lights in our masks turned on, Wolf and I can see just a few feet ahead. We walk carefully but not too slowly. We don't want to spend more time here than we need to.

We walk and walk, looking for the place where I saw the puppy. Up the hill, under a bush. That seems like it could be anywhere. The night is quiet. Even if we do find the puppy, how will we find Jack again? We didn't think to leave any trail or markers, and even if we'd thought of it—what would we have left?

The puppy was up the hill, under a bush. Just remember that, Nano, and be smart. But through the plants, the palms, the thorny bushes, the night, it's hard to see where a hill would be. So we just walk, and I hope.

I can now hear dogs snuffling, yipping. My skin feels tingly, my heart races. *We're close*, I think. A little more, and there's the hill. I point it out to Wolf, who nods. As we walk up it, I feel triumphant. Just need to find the right bush. Just need to get out of here, with the puppy.

Something runs past us, lightning fast, just grazing the side of my leg. Then here it comes again, this time knocking Wolf down onto the ground. The dog—who must be seventy pounds, covered in thick, luscious brown fur—stands on Wolf's chest and stares into his face.

"Don't hurt him," I whisper. "Please don't hurt him."

The dog sniffs Wolf's whole face so slowly. His mouth, his nose—I hope his dog suit is doing what it is supposed to do. I hold my breath. I can hear Wolf whimper. I will him to be quiet, to not give more clues that we don't belong.

The dog opens his mouth, wide, and leans down. He picks up the ear on the dog mask, closes his mouth and tears it off in one fast motion, then runs off with the ear in his mouth. There is a hole now, in his mask, where the ear should be. Wolf's human scent will come through. Now I'm not sure whether to hope George can or can't see us on the monitor, if we need rescuing. I do know we'd better do this fast.

"Look under all the bushes," I instruct Wolf. We move from one large plant to the next, looking for a puppy. None, none, none. For all I know, the puppy's gone anyway. Walked off, been killed and eaten. I pretend those aren't howls we're hearing.

Finally, I hear a rustle. I kneel down. There's the puppy. Oh, thank Dog, thank *Dog*.

I reach under the bush to pick up the puppy. The puppy makes a kind of squeak when I lift it—I check, it's a him. He looks so scared. I kiss the top of his head through my mask.

"You're going to be okay," I promise him, in no position to make that promise. He immediately pees on me. Luckily, the dog suit is water-repellent.

"C'mon," I say to Wolf. "We'd better get back fast."

I carry the puppy, who is so light that he barely registers in my arms. Wolf and I walk as fast as we can in what I am hopeful is the right direction, if I am reading the stars right, if I am remembering right, which I hope I am. I am mindful not to drop the puppy, who has begun to chew on my mask, which moves the eyeholes, which makes it hard to see, which makes it hard not to fall, which makes it hard not to drop him.

"Quit it, tiny," I whisper in his ear. "I'm trying to save you."

I'm sure I hear dogs chasing us as we make our way back to the beach. There are howls, there are rustles, but we encounter no dogs. I hope to Dog that George isn't looking at the right monitor, that the Internet is on the fritz, whatever breakdown we need for this to work.

When we get to the fence, I have no idea where we are but it seems safest to climb over and worry about the kayaks after.

"You go first," I instruct Wolf. He leaps onto the fence. I reach up to hand him the puppy. When Wolf touches the puppy, we both get a terrible jolt.

Wolf falls off the fence. He drops the puppy. I cry out and rush to make sure that he—the puppy—is okay. He is on the ground, still. I grab him, I hold him; I check his breathing.

I listen for his heartbeat. I can't tell if he is even alive. Oh, to think that we might have taken this risk, deprived him of a painless death, only to make him suffer—I can't bear to think it.

Now he's wriggling just a bit, just enough to let me know he's still here. Thank Dog, thank *Dog*, thank Dog.

Wolf hops back onto the fence. This time I know not to hand him the puppy because that completes the circuit and leads to us all being shocked. I toss the puppy as softly as I can, instead. But it's too softly, and Wolf can't catch him. I catch him on the way down, then toss him a little higher, a little harder, and for a second it looks like the puppy might just fly, then fall, but Wolf reaches out. He catches the puppy with one hand, while holding onto the fence with his other. The puppy barks, growls. It's very cute, in this scary moment.

I leap up, too. Scramble up fast.

"Hand him to me," I say, when I reach the top. He does. I clutch the puppy to myself as I carefully navigate my way over the barbed wire, back down the other side. Wolf jumps down to join me. We start whisper-yelling for Jack, who responds in a normal tone of voice.

"Right here," he says, here being surprisingly close by.

We walk to Jack. He is standing, looking serious. The puppy growls at him, but Jack doesn't seem to mind. He looks like he's just witnessed a miracle. Which in a way, I guess he has.

"This is him," I say. It feels overwhelming. It feels like everything is changing, has changed. "Here he is."

"Dog be with you," Jack says. "Dog be with you, little one."

WE PADDLE BACK TO the beach quietly. The puppy sits in my kayak. I worry the whole way that we will tip over, he will fall in, he will drown, I will lose him. If I have some nervousness, still, that he might be wild and vicious, this goes away when he falls asleep, his little body rising and falling with every deep breath. My heart hurts, looking at him.

Back at shore, we put the kayaks back where they belong.

"I'll go get some food," says Jack. He heads off to the cafeteria for supplies, for the puppy and for us.

Wolf builds a small fire, near a private corner of the beach, by some tall rocks and tall palms. The warmth feels good. I take off my dog mask, sitting there. The puppy looks confused for a moment, then snaps at me, biting my cheek with sharp teeth. I wipe my cheek with the back of my dog-suited hand, and there is blood on the fabric. I put my dog mask back on. The puppy sniffs me again, then rolls over on his back. I rub his belly. His hind leg shakes, just like he's a robot dog.

Wolf rubs my belly, while I rub the puppy's. I shake my leg. Wolf laughs. I love to hear him laugh, love to make him laugh.

The puppy bites his hand.

"Ow!" he says.

"Wait till he gets big," I say, first jokingly, then not. What will happen once he gets big? Even medium? There aren't a lot of *plans* in place just yet. Well, that'll come. I suppose that'll come. The puppy has fallen asleep with his back paw in his mouth. I remove my mask. He makes some squeaking noises, some little snores.

Wolf rubs his hand all over me. "Your dog suit feels nice," he says. "You should wear it a lot." I smile.

"I, um. Here's some food," says Jack. He throws a couple of packets of dehydrated pea snacks at us and unwraps four CowFree patties. He puts them on rolls, applies slices of vegan cheese on top, and hands one to me, Wolf, and the puppy. The puppy wakes up, growls, and then gobbles down the burger. Jack gives the puppy a second helping, which he also dispatches quickly.

"You mind?" Jack asks me, pointing at the burger I am holding in my hands. (Wolf has already finished his.)

"Of course not," I say, despite being starving. The puppy looks at me, unmasked, bares his teeth, and then takes the burger. He wags his tail while growling when he's done.

Jack leaves for more provisions, returns with donuts. "I think your dad made a bunch of them for group dinner tonight. I don't know why there are leftovers," he says, then takes a bite, spits it out. "Yeah, I know why there are leftovers."

"Donut," I say.

Jack hands me one. "It's not good, though."

The puppy eats it from my hand. His body is mostly black, but he has white legs with spots on them. His face is mostly white with a black mask. It makes him look like a miniature (furry) superhero. His ears are long and floppy. "I mean as a name. Donut. 'Cause he's small and sweet."

The puppy finishes the donut then bites my nose.

"Not so sweet," Wolf observes.

"Don't listen to mean Wolf," I murmur. His fur is so soft.

The three of us take turns sleeping that night, on a secluded part of the beach, by the fire, with Donut, who snores and whimpers, and growls in his sleep, and twitches his feet as he seems to dream. I think we all know, without saying, that this might be the last easy time we have.

CHAPTER 5

In the morning, Jack fetches more food and some coffee pills from the cafeteria, and some water for Donut. Wolf watches Donut while I go off to pee at the public toilet near the Casino, where I can see that folks are gathering to set up for the Marky Barky party tonight. (The Casino isn't for gambling. It's a 150-year-old building, from back when Beachport was a fishing village and tourist town. They had dances and weddings and stuff here. It's where we have all our important events now. The building's been repainted for Marky Barky's party, its bright turquoise exterior just a shade more vibrant than the Gulf.)

"He bit me but not too hard," Wolf tells me, when I come back. "He's a little bit of a knucklehead."

"You are," I say. "Don't talk about my puppy like that." Donut starts racing around in circles, like a crazy idiot. Running, stopping, crouching, yipping, starting up again. It is so funny. I've never seen anything like this before. I wish we could put a bubble around ourselves and never have to move.

Jack returns, carrying Mr. Chi-Chi Pants. "I ran into your dad. He was worried you didn't come home," he says.

"What did you tell him?"

"That we camped out."

"Did he seem mad?" I ask.

"No," he says. "Just said you should go home and ask Ruby what she needs help with. Apparently she has a huge surprise waiting for you."

"Judy and Peter are probably wondering as to my whereabouts, too," says Wolf.

"Yeah," Jack says. "Mom was glad and mad to see me."

We confer. Tomorrow, we decide, we can develop a long-term plan about just what in the hell we are going to do now. For now, there's just the matter of figuring out how to navigate today—which shouldn't be too hard, we optimistically agree, since most of Dog Island will be too distracted by Marky Barky's impending arrival to think much about our whereabouts.

We can't be too far from the action, since we will be needed, but we've got to be somewhere we won't be seen. There's only one real option, given those parameters, and it's The Smiling Manatee—an old tiki bar that's upstairs from a restaurant that officially went out of business thirteen years ago. It's got broken old neon signs hanging on the walls and a balcony from which you can see the Casino and the beach.

I know this because sometimes people in their twenties who intern here or move here for a while, or forever, have (not so) secret parties there (and sometimes they invite us— they all seem to like Wolf a lot). Wolf gets drunk at the parties and winds up dancing like a maniac all night; Jack ends up in some long conversation about, like, the history of flag symbols or how the drought stimulated a micro-boom in sustainable agriculture. I usually end up standing by the balcony with my robot dog, one eye on the party and the other on the water. Anyway, I'm familiar with the place, is my point.

We hide Donut in the tote bag that Jack used to carry our food and walk across the beach trying to be invisible. But no luck. Here comes Marjorie on her one-speed bicycle, her macaw, Harold, perched on the handlebars, while the pair embark on their morning constitutional. Marjorie waves hello. Harold raises a wing in greeting.

Marjorie is in her eighties. So is Harold. She dresses as if she is a macaw herself—reds and blues and yellows, all flowy fabrics. She's always asking who will assume Harold's care when she dies. He will probably live to be 150 years old. She will hopefully live to be ninety.

Everyone tries to assure her that Dog Island will not let Harold be without care. Several people have volunteered so far, but Marjorie keeps finding reasons to reject them.

Dorothy holds up Harold's uncertain fate as one enormous reason why keeping live animals—as opposed to robot dogs—as pets is not allowed on Dog Island. According to her, it is "immoral and fraught" and should be discouraged if not outright banned in society at large. Harold got grandfathered into living here, since he and Marjorie were here before Dorothy instituted the pet ban.

"Shalom, kids!" she calls out, stopping. "Are you coming to help set up?"

"Yes, soon!" I say. Dear Dog, please stay quiet, please stay quiet. "Will Harold be pitching in?"

Marjorie guffaws. "He'll supervise."

"I'll supervise!" Harold shouts. "I'll supervise! Who's a good bird?"

"Not you," says Marjorie. "You are just terrible, Harold." She cackles and he shrieks as they ride off.

"They make a good couple," Jack observes. "I hope one day I'm that happy."

"Oh, don't worry, buddy. There's no chance you will be that happy," says Wolf. He kisses my cheek.

Wolf goes up to stay with Donut first, while Jack and I head our separate ways to our respective homes.

I am hoping that no one will be there. It would sure be great to sit down for a moment, have a bite to eat, and reflect. But no such luck. Instead, I arrive to find my mom entertaining Marky Barky himself.

"Oh!" I say, when I spot the movie star sitting on a shabby wicker couch in my living room. "What are you doing here?"

He laughs, giving me those trademark crinkle-edged eyes, and runs a hand through his thick salt-and-pepper hair.

"Your mother invited us," he says. Mom nods, giggling.

My robot dog Billy comes dashing over to me and sits at my feet. I didn't know he could move that fast. He has an unusually large smile on his face. What, he's starstruck, too?

"Where were you last night, Nano?" Mom asks.

I blush. "I was at the beach with Wolf and Jack."

"You forgot how to use your phone?"

"I wasn't getting a signal," I say.

"I see," Mom says. "Mr. Barky. Mr. Hot Bod, if you will.

What would you do if your daughter failed to come home one night?"

Kill me. Kill me now. Only don't because then I won't get to go back and take care of Donut. Or see Wolf.

"Oh, he doesn't give a crap," says a girl coming in from the kitchen. I immediately recognize her as Ellie, Marky Barky's daughter, who is about five years older than me, and a million times more sophisticated. She's wearing some kind of attractive but casual dress and black boots. They're materials that are different from what I usually see here. They look, I don't know how to put it exactly, *expensive*, I guess. Her hair—which is not butt length, or buzz cut, or a choppy bob, or a stupid glamour style—is silver and blue and tied up perfectly on top of her head. She looks so *cool*.

Ellie and I used to play when I was really little, and she was young enough to find me interesting, and she'd come with Marky Barky on his yearly visit. Then at some point she lost interest in me but discovered an interest in my brother Billy. The two of them would go disappear to do—well, stuff, I suppose? Sex stuff, maybe? It feels embarrassing to think about. Then I guess that also stopped being what she wanted to do anymore, and for the last five or so years she hasn't accompanied Marky Barky on his Dog Island visits.

"That's not true, Ellie. I definitely give a crap," says Marky Barky.

"I know, Dad. I'm just kidding." Then, to me: "I was told you'd be providing me some entertainment?"

"Oh!" I say. Wolf would be much better at this. "Mom, don't you need me to help set up?"

"No, you girls just go have some fun," says Mom.

I feel vexed. On the one hand, there are important things I really need to be doing that I can't do while I have to take care of Ellie. And also, what are we supposed to actually do? I spend every single day of my life here and can't think of a single thing to do that might be fun to the daughter of Marky Barky. What, are we going to play Bionic Woman? What if she wants to be Max the dog?

"Here, let's go for a walk," Ellie says to me, taking my hand and leading me to the front door. I had been planning to go brush my teeth, change my clothes, charge my phone, eat some food, take a couple more coffee pills, and figure out what in the hell we are going to do with and about Donut, and so on.

I sneak a look at Marky Barky. His face looks relaxed and friendly, and impassive. And handsome. My Dog, I see why he's called Hot Bod. I wonder if he and Dorothy really are "lovers." Ew.

What can I do? I follow Ellie. Billy trots beside.

"It's hot," she says, when we get outside. "I don't know how you live like this."

"I could lend you some paw protectors if you want to change out of your boots," I suggest. She shakes her head no, while wrinkling her nose. I push her on this issue a little, since being hot and wearing boots seem like a dumb combination. Plus, what's wrong with paw protectors? They are very comfortable and functional. She keeps turning me down, and I give up. As Dorothy says, "You can lead a robot horse to water, but you can't make it drink because robots don't drink water, which is just one of the many ways they are superior to Organics."

"Want to go to the library?" I suggest. "It's small, but it's got air-conditioning and we can watch a movie or read."

She shakes her head no. "I'm in grad school now," she says. "In New York. I don't feel like I need a trip to the Dog Island Library, thanks."

"There's an old arcade," I say. "Some pinball machines. It's also air-conditioned, sort of."

"That sounds kind of stupid," she says. "Can't we visit the sanctuary? I haven't been in *years*."

"The Ruffuge?" I ask.

"Oy," she says. "The dog puns. Yes, the Ruffuge."

"I think Dorothy is planning to take you and your dad to see the dogs tomorrow," I say.

"Aren't there any other dogs I could see?"

My heart feels like it's stopped.

"Of course not," I say. "Except the robot dogs."

She looks at Billy. "I don't understand why they keep making these stupid machines. No one cares about them anymore."

I pull out my phone and press "positive interaction" because hearing her say this makes me feel extremely guilty.

Then I remember: it's just a robot, anyway, so who cares what she says. I also decline to report a couple of live cats that Billy points out to me.

"What are you studying?" I ask, while we stroll. Sweat is pouring off Ellie's face, and she is flushed but still looks fantastic.

"Bioethics," she says.

"Oh yeah?" I ask. "That sounds hard."

"It's the most important thing in the world. How we ought to behave toward living things," she says to me. "I think you'd like it."

I feel a wave of, I don't know, gratitude and surprise. Ellie is taking an interest in me. I relax a little bit.

"Do you want to go to the arcade?" I ask.

"Not really," she says. "But okay."

We walk over to the Beachport Play N Snack, which is not an accurate name anymore because there are no snacks. The titular "play" is just a couple of old pinball machines and arcade games no one bothered to get rid of. My brother, Billy, and I used to come hang out here, like if it was raining out or too hot and we just wanted something to do. Wolf and Jack and I come sometimes, too. We think it's fun. Maybe really it's super lame. Maybe Ellie and Billy used to come here, way back when.

Arriving, Ellie seems pleased. "I forgot that this place is so retro," she says approvingly, approaching the Twilight Zone pinball machine. She presses some buttons, seems engaged in the game, and then it's done.

I'm playing the Ms. Pac-Man machine, eating digital dots, outrunning ghosts. I can do this all day, and have from time to time. But Ellie comes and stands behind me, very close, looking over my shoulder, and it makes me so nervous that I basically commit Ms. Pac-Man suicide just to get out of this.

"What else is there to do?" she asks. We've been hanging out for less than an hour.

I sigh heavily. "You want to go robot horse riding?" I ask. "The robot horses might be working okay now. I think Wolf was fixing them. They're old and nothing special. You probably have much better ones in California, but . . ."

"Can we see the dogs?" she asks. "Or any dog?"

"Oh, I still don't think so," I say. I laugh nervously. "Just the robots."

"Ugh. No. Well what do *you* do for fun here?" she asks.

"Hang out with Wolf and Jack mostly."

"Are they cute?" she asks. I feel my face heating up. "Oh my god, are you *blushing*?"

"No," I say.

"Okay, so obviously they are cute enough to make you turn into a tomato. Let's go find them."

I have never actually seen a real tomato and am in fact curious to hear more about what they look and taste like, but I am not about to volunteer that information. Thus I find myself being led around *my* Dog Island by Marky Barky's cool daughter, to look for my pals. I of course can't take her to the place where at least one of them actually is, for obvious reasons. Wolf might still be at home, or else he's at the Casino helping to set up. Ellie and I first stop by his house, which is on the way to the Casino. He wasn't lying; it's really bright green now. I open the front door—no one locks doors here—and call out but no one answers.

Then we walk over to and down Beach Boulevard, past the couple of mostly empty shops and cafes, the yoga studio-cum-beauty salon-cum-tattoo parlor. These have managed to stay open mostly thanks to visitors who arrive here with some money to spend and the urge for a permanent souvenir. (Dorothy subsidizes them during lean years because she loves them or loves their proprietors, and because she likes knowing there are Dog Island tats in the outside word.)

We venture into the Casino, where the adults are in various states of meltdown.

"Where are my tablecloths?" Owen, who plans all our events, is shouting. "WHERE ARE MY CENTERPIECES?" He has been having this same meltdown since I was seven, when he first moved to the sanctuary.

Ellie and I decamp to the other side of the Casino, before Owen starts up again. Mom is there on a ladder, affixing dog-print fabric to the wall in an attractive and festive manner.

"Oh shalom, girls," says Mom. "Whatcha up to? Going kayaking?"

Ellie squints at Mom's decorations. "That needs to be higher to look right."

"You think so?" Mom asks, adopting Ellie's same expression while gazing at the wall she's working on prettifying. She rips the cloth off the wall and goes on her tiptoes to hold it up a little higher. "Oh my Dog, girlfriend. You are so right!"

Ugh, Mom.

"Good," Ellie says, and starts walking out of the Casino toward the beach, her boots making loud clomping noises as she walks.

"She's a spitfire!" says Mom. "What are you going to do with her now?"

"I honestly don't know," I say.

"I'm sure you'll think of something!" Mom trills. "Maybe she wants to help us set up! We have a lot of work to do and she has a good eye."

"Yeah, she seems eager to help," I say. "Seems like she's all about helping."

I go trotting after Ellie, who has exited the Casino and is now sitting on some steps leading to the beach. She's slipped on a pair of sunglasses and is looking out toward the water. I'm so busy noticing her looking *even more amazing* that at first I fail to take in what she's looking at.

It's Wolf, who is holding court.

"That's Wolf," I say. I smile. I can't help it.

"Oh, he's cute. I definitely want to meet him," she says.

We walk over. "Hey," I say to him nervously. How will things be now? To think, a year ago we were just friends; a day ago we hadn't embarked on a cockamamie puppy rescue mission. I'm probably overthinking things; Wolf beams at me, kisses my cheek. I smile up at him.

There's a small group of Dog Islanders nearby, smoking cigarettes, gossiping, avoiding setting up the Casino. They're some of the Bad Bitches.

One of them, Patricia, calls out, "Ooh, ooh! You two will get married here in the Casino one day. I hope I live to help decorate for it!" The others start to laugh.

"I'm Ellie," says Ellie, holding her hand out to Wolf. "I think last time I met you, you were eight years old. You look a lot different now. So you two are . . ."

"Yeah," Wolf says. "We totally are." He puts his arm around my shoulders. I'm so happy.

"How *adorable*," she says.

Wolf asks me: "Hey, have you checked on Jack, and, you know?"

I elbow him in the side.

"Ow! All I asked was if you checked . . ." I elbow him again.

"You aren't very subtle, kid," Ellie says to me. "Let's go check on Jack. I bet he's cute, too."

"No," I say.

"He's not cute?"

"Yeah," says Wolf. "Do you not think our Jack is cute?"

"Wolf, just go," I say to him.

He kisses me on the lips, for maybe like two hours, then walks off toward The Smiling Manatee. Ellie watches him.

"He's adorable," she says to me. Then she asks where the bathroom is. I point out the public restrooms, just across the street, explaining they haven't been cleaned yet but will be before the party tonight.

"It's fine," she says. "I'll be right back."

There she goes, clomping to and then into the bathroom. I drift off a little, while she's there. I'm thinking about Donut, mostly. I try to search my mind, to figure out why I felt the need to take him. And in so doing, to create a massive, possibly devastating complication in my life. If we get caught . . . I don't have an answer. I know it could be extremely bad. Then I think of his face, looking into mine. I think of his tail, wagging. I know it was the right thing to do.

After a while, I realize it's been a long time since Ellie went to the bathroom. Look, I get it, sometimes your stomach hurts. But maybe I should check on her. See if she needs me to get her something, like more toilet paper. (The public bathrooms are sparsely stocked, since TP is a hot commodity that frequently gets stolen for personal use. Dorothy likes to say that "toilet paper *does* grow on trees, but these magnificent creations of nature are in short supply, and they aren't ours to cut down, depriving animals of their habitat." We are encouraged to use a reusable cloth instead of the paper, and while some go along with this plan, many of us find it disgusting beyond measure.)

She's not in there. There are only two stalls, both are empty of Ellie (and of toilet paper).

I search the beach, the Casino, the little main drag where perhaps she is taking a stroll, but no Ellie. "Where is she?" I ask my robot dog, who does not answer—it would be shocking if he did.

Well, I think, I lost Marky Barky's daughter, but it could be worse. Now at least I can go relieve Jack of his Donut duties for a bit, maybe make out with Wolf for a while. Spend time with the puppy, plot our next steps.

Looking around to make sure no one's watching, I walk up the cracked concrete steps, to The Smiling Manatee. At the top of the stairs, past the swinging door, there's Jack and Mr. Chi-Chi Pants. There's Wolf. There's Donut.

And crap on a spoon, there's Ellie.

We at Mechanical Tail are DELIGHTED to announce a brand-new trade-in program. Because our ROBOT DOGS are so well-crafted, they will be by your side forever!

But wouldn't you like to try out our exciting new models? Now you can! Simply send back your OLD model robot dog using one of our prepaid return boxes. We will credit you half the cost of your NEW AND IMPROVED ROBOT BEST FRIEND!

CHAPTER 6

You have these moments. Something bad is happening, or just happened, or is about to happen. And your mind, rather than dealing with what is before you, starts imagining other scenarios, in which this bad thing is avoided.

In this alternate scenario, I am imagining that Ellie did not come to Dog Island with her father, the movie star Marky Barky. I am imagining that we'd chosen a better place to hide out, with the puppy. Or that I went with Ellie to the bathroom and prevented her from entering The Smiling Manatee. Or even that she got run over by a GoPod and had to be Air-Vaxed to the hospital.

But here we are.

Donut's sleeping next to Jack, who is sitting on the floor, watching all this with a distant look on his face. Ellie bends down and picks him up—Donut, not Jack. He yawns, yips, and licks her nose. I feel a little angry and confused; she's not even wearing a dog suit.

"This doesn't seem well planned out you guys," Ellie observes. "What are you planning to do, just live here in this empty tiki bar with the illegal dog?"

She holds the puppy like a baby in her arms. He just lies there chewing on his own paws, as if this is normal, but none of it is normal.

"But really. What is your plan?"

We don't answer. What could we say?

"You guys, this is serious," she says. "No shitting around. Unless the rules have changed, you are not supposed to have a puppy. And that's why you are hiding in this filthy, disgusting tiki bar that appears not even to have any booze, which would have been its only redeeming feature?"

"That's more or less accurate," I say.

With that crack in the floodgate, Ellie asks more questions and more questions still. She draws the story out of us. I hear myself describing and defending what we've done, telling her how we saved Donut's life, how they were going to kill him, how he's not supposed to be alive at all, but look at him, *look at him,* his tail wags. It wags. It wags. Dog tails don't do that, but his does.

"I can see," she says. "It's pretty amazing. Like change-the-world amazing."

I feel excitement and dread at her words. Dread and anxiety at the next ones.

"I think you should let me take him," she says.

"No. No chance," Jack says, before I have a chance to say another word.

Ellie smiles, in a way that doesn't look exactly friendly. Her teeth are very white. She probably has more than just a tele-dentist and robot dental assistant giving her cleanings and checkups. "I could just take him. I don't think there's a lot you could do about it, frankly. But, guys, friends, let me try to convince you this is the better plan. There's something I want to show you. Tonight, you'll come with me. I think you will find it interesting. Besides, have you even ever been to Disney?"

No, we haven't. Because it shut down ten years ago, and even before then our families had no money, no way of getting there, and so on.

"What are you even talking about?" Wolf says.

"Just come. Bring Donut. Trust me. And even if you don't trust me . . ."

Ellie hands me Donut, then takes a picture of us with her phone, and snaps a couple more of the inside of The Smiling Manatee. Tells us to meet her at 9 P.M., at this park about three blocks from the Casino. She'll have a PlaneCab waiting.

"Bye!" she says, walking out, her boots loud on the tile, down the stairs.

I guess "shell-shocked" might be the best word to describe how I feel. Jack, Wolf, and I confer. Our options, as we see them, aren't fantastic, to put it mildly.

Theoretically we could put Donut back in the Ruffuge, somehow, perhaps. Where, for sure, he'll be picked up and killed when the dinner shift comes through, if he stays alive even that long. Another idea is for us to go and hide, with him. The downside to this is that there is literally no place on Dog Island where we could do that for the long term—and getting away isn't so possible either, seeing as we have no boat or plane . . .

"Maybe she's right," Wolf says. "She seems pretty nice. And she's rich. So that's good."

"The person who just blackmailed us? You think she seems *nice?*" Jack says.

They start whisper-yelling at each other, back and forth and back and forth. Billy my robot dog stands close by.

"Guys," I finally say. "Guys! What can we do?"

"End his suffering right now," says Jack. "That's what we could do. What we should have done in the first place." He glares at the puppy, at us. I think he might be crying. I don't know why he helped, if this is how he feels.

We *could* go steal some Kinderend from my mom. Donut would be no worse off; he would be at peace. We probably couldn't bring his body to the chapel because it would be noticeable if we light the furnace. So we could bury him or send him off to sea. Give him and ourselves peace. But I can't. My heart hurts to think of it.

"So how about this," I propose. "How about we get the Kinderend? We bring it with us, tonight. If things get bad, if we don't like what's happening . . ."

"I already don't like what's happening," says Jack. But he agrees. Wolf agrees. We all agree, except Donut, whose fate is entirely outside his own hands, or paws.

We spend the day together, up in The Smiling Manatee. Sitting on the floor, me leaning against Wolf, Jack's head in my lap, as he smokes so much weed. Donut sometimes sleeps against my leg, sometimes runs in circles around the room— his little nails clacking against the tile. My robot dog Billy watches, as if he is truly taking in what Donut is and what he is doing. If he had a brain, which he doesn't, it would be odd for him to know that this puppy is what he was built to replace.

Every once in a while one of us leaves to get more food and water for Donut, to check on what's happening at the Casino, see if they need us, make sure Ellie isn't there stirring up trouble. I see, on these visits, that she is spending the day sunbathing, as the fuss and stress goes on around her.

I go home in the late afternoon to charge my phone, give myself a Sani-Fresh wipe down, and collect the Kinderend. It's in the Parents' Room, in a small safe that Mom thinks I don't know the code to. Except it's the same code she uses for everything: 7829, the numbers that correspond to RUBY, her name. She has five containers of Kinderend in the safe; I take just one.

Then there's the issue of what to wear. My clothes don't really fit anymore, because of my newish boobs. I meant to print out a new dress but forgot to do it on time (and you always have to leave at least two hours to print out a new article of clothing since the printer gets jammed, you lose the Internet connection, etc. etc. etc.).

I check Mom's closet. Her dresses are dazzlingly bad— most accomplish the (you'd think) impossible feat of being flamboyant and dowdy at the same time. I've selected a dress that is made of a shiny silver material and floor-length on me. This one manages to both be a little too tight (in the chest) and to look like a sack (everywhere else). But it's a pretty color and long enough that I can wear paw protectors instead of real shoes, and it has pockets, which I can slip the Kinderend into, so it will be close at hand.

"Do I look all right?" I ask my robot dog Billy. He picks up a toy from the floor and holds it near my hands. We play a little tug-of-war, which is fun—it's what I know people used to do with the Organic dogs, back when they had them as pets—but then I stop given how tight the dress is on my boobs; I'm worried about ripping this stupid dress.

I sit on the bed a second, then lie down and look at the ceiling. It's got water stains and a funky old ceiling fan that realistically could come crashing down any second. Billy hops up onto the bed with me and tries to rest his head on me. I should shove him away; I don't want to get his "fur" on the dress. I feel like so much is out of my control, and I just want to look okay/nice at least. I rub his belly and he shakes his leg. I like this feature. People must have been sad when they couldn't do this with the Organic dogs anymore.

Mom and Dad come back to the house. They must not know I'm here because they are using their flirty "we're all alone and in love" voices with each other.

Dad to Mom: "Tell me the truth. Am I as handsome as Hot Bod?"

Mom to Dad: "Even better. Your hiney is Oscar-worthy." Then: "Oh Saul. I miss him so much."

Dad to Mom: "Please, Ruby. Not now. Can't we focus on my tight buns, please?"

Mom to Dad: "How about you get yourself out of those pants and I take a closer look?"

I pop out of their room to interrupt before this conversation can proceed to a very woeful place.

"I'm here," I say.

"My beautiful daughter!" Mom cries out. "Aren't you a vision? And just look how that old dress of mine highlights your lovely bosom! I can't believe how grown you are!" She takes my hands and stares at my chest. "Saul, can you believe we *made* this child? Two beautiful, perfect children."

Dad, thanks be to the Dogs, is quiet on this matter.

Obviously I would love to go put on a different dress now. But—I finger what's in my pocket. It would be hard to transfer the tube of Kinderend without anyone noticing. Also, there is no surfeit of less bosom-y dresses at my disposal. And third, maybe Wolf will like me in this dress. It's possible. Weirder, much weirder, things have happened and are happening.

I could tell Mom and Dad about these things. Right now. They could maybe help me get out of the trouble we're in. But I think I know where that goes: it goes to Donut dying.

"I'm going to head back over to the Casino," I say. "See you there?"

"Dog be with you!" trills Mom. She's in such a good mood, I think a little bitterly. Does she even remember that it was just after the party last year that we lost Billy?

I rush back to The Smiling Manatee. Jack is still there. He's smoking more weed, he's playing with Donut—holding out his hand, teasing the puppy, who lunges in for a bite then seems surprised when Jack quickly pulls his hand away.

"We've been doing this for a couple of hours," Jack tells me. "The vicious beastie doesn't get tired of this game."

"Has he eaten?" I ask.

Jack says yes, Wolf brought over some food not too long ago. Then he asks me if I "brought the stuff."

I pat my pocket, say yeah, and sit down on the dirty floor, no longer caring about the stupid dress.

"I've been wanting to ask you something," Jack says to me.

"What?" I ask.

He pauses. "Forget it. You know they're taking Mr. Chi-Chi Pants tomorrow."

"Yeah," I say. My last moments with Derrick are right there with me, in a flash. "We're so special. Don't you feel special?"

He reaches over and takes my hand. I feel a jolt, like I did at the fence, but pull it away.

"Wolf . . ." I say.

"Wolf," he repeats. "Sure. Of course."

Just then, the actual Wolf appears, as if we'd conjured him. He is wearing a Hawaiian shirt with some perma-cotton pants. His hair looks freshly combed.

"You look like crap," Wolf says to Jack. "Go home and wash your face."

"Aye, aye, asshole," Jack says. He has a bit of a hard time lifting himself up off the floor, but makes it, and shakes his legs out.

"We're finally alone," Wolf says, once Jack is gone. I smile. Not quite alone, I point out, nodding toward Donut, who is looking quizzically up at us.

We can hear from here that the band is getting started over at the Casino. The Dog Island Coco-Nuts; they play at every party. Oldies and rock, mostly—stuff that was out-of-date even when these musicians were growing up. They're playing "Hard to Handle" now, which will be followed by "I Will Survive" because it always is. The set list never changes.

I bend down, scoop up Donut. Wolf puts his arms around

the two of us. Sways back and forth a little. My dog, I will miss this, this thing that is so new and precious. I want to preserve it in amber, to put it behind glass. I want to keep living it and feeling it forever.

Jack returns. He's spruced up a little. His hair is quite crispy.

"It's time to go over," he says. "Almost seven."

We settle on half-hour shifts. Me first, here. The two guys leave. Donut and I stay back. I watch them go; I can see the sun setting over the horizon. It's so beautiful and over so quickly. Wolf comes to relieve me of my duties, in no time.

I head across the street to the Casino. The party is underway, with everyone in their loud, skin-baring fancy clothes, already getting buzzy on this year's signature drink.

Dad invented it: the Dog-quiri. The recipe calls for coconut, sugar, and lime, blended with almost-ice and a generous amount of rum, and topped with a dog-printed umbrella. Once he'd experimented with the boozy possibilities for months and settled on this cocktail for the event, Mom pointed out to him that this drink is just a regular daiquiri, but with the dog-printed umbrella.

"Classic!" Dad exclaimed, and it was so good to see him feeling enthusiastic about something that, sure, Mom mocked him for his lack of creativity for fifteen or twenty minutes more, but you could tell her heart wasn't in it.

She held his hand, after a bit, and said, "I'm sure they'll be a big success. Even if they are terribly derivative." Dad smiled.

I'm looking around for Jack but don't see him. People say hello to me on their way to and from the bar, or outside to the beach to smoke. I spot Ellie on the other side of the room. She's with her dad, the movie star Marky Barky, both of them mobbed. They both look so gorgeous. He is in a tuxedo with a dog-print tie and cummerbund. She's in a bright green dress. They are both smiling. How can she smile right now? I can't imagine. I can't imagine blackmailing a group of people, threatening the things that mean the most to them, then putting on a pretty dress and being bright and shiny at a party. I feel so angry all of a sudden.

Dorothy's voice comes over the loudspeaker: "Please be seated, Dog Islanders! You are about to be entertained, enthralled, impressed! You will not want to miss a single second!"

She has a magnificent voice. Raspy and a tiny bit wry, with a touch of a babyish lisp. Wise and fresh at the same time. People are always surprised the first time they hear Dorothy speak. Then they want to hear every single thing she has to say.

There's no official assigned seating here, but we all basically sit in the same places every event, every year. Same crowd, same chatter, usually I love it.

The lights go dim. Dorothy's voice comes back over the loudspeaker. "Reach under your seats," she orders.

I feel around, wondering what surprise is in store. There's a soft little sack down there. Seems to be attached by Velcro. I tear it away.

Inside are a pair of glasses and some headphones. I slip them on. Everyone around me is doing the same.

I blink twice, adjusting to a shock of colors and shapes, the noises I somehow hear in my brain but not in my ears. I feel myself drifting into a kind of trance, and then suddenly there is an explosion of fireworks, magnificent fireworks. I see them and hear them so crisply—but I also *feel* them, somehow. As if I am inside the display instead of witnessing the fireworks from below.

These fireworks are hot pink and shiny gold, fluorescent yellow and mint green. They go off in the usual beautiful bursts but also form trees and shells and flowers and all kinds of different things. And you don't just see the big shapes, you can see each individual firework. They're each shaped like a dog! A tiny, sparkly, three-dimensional dog. This is new and wonderful! I reach out my hand to touch one, but of course there's nothing to touch. It's all an illusion, a beautiful illusion.

"Now take off your glasses," Dorothy commands, telling us that she will unveil this year's robot dog in just a minute.

"His name," she says, "is Handsome Hank, and he has several extremely exciting new features thanks to our friends at Mechanical Tail."

"He is waterproof!" she cries out. "And comes in four different sizes!" Now, I'm imagining what this sounds like to Ellie. *No one cares about robot dogs*, she'd said. I look at my robot dog Billy. Mentally tell him: This is what they are replacing you with, buddy, pretty soon. This is why I'm not getting too attached. My next one will be waterproof. He looks at me as if he can read my mind, as if he even has thoughts or feelings, and wags his tail a little, stiffly.

You're an "it" and nothing more than an "it," I think. Donut is real.

I stealthily check my phone; yep, already late for my next shift. Dorothy is launching into her introduction of "our most special guest, Mr. Hot Bod himself, the one and only Marky Barky."

"I have to pee," I whisper to Mom, leaving. Billy follows me away. I snatch some appetizers off platters on my way out of the Casino.

Upstairs, at The Smiling Manatee, Wolf is pacing the room.

"Is the party fun?" he asks me.

"It's okay," I say. "Dorothy was introducing the new robot dog when I left."

"Good new features?"

"Waterproof. Some other stuff . . ."

I tell Wolf to go back to the Casino so that no one notices him being gone. I feed some of the food to Donut. Eat some of it myself. Tastes all right; thanks Dad. It's getting to be almost nine, almost time.

Wolf and Jack, holding Mr. Chi-Chi Pants, come back up. We give each other sad smiles. I finagle Donut back into the tote bag. I don't know how many times our luck can hold, carrying him around like this. Hopefully at least once more.

We quietly walk downstairs. My arms are bare and chilly. I have goose bumps; maybe it's nerves. We start walking toward the park, but the silence is quickly interrupted.

"Kids! Kids! Where have you been?" It's Mom, vigorously waving her arm. "We've all been looking for you. Did you want to get your picture taken with Marky Barky?"

"No, that's okay," I say.

"Come on. Come *on*! Stop being such a stick-in-the-mud! I want a picture of me and my beautiful daughter and the even more beautiful Hot Bod!" She reaches over to grab me by the arm, and I just *know* that Donut is going to be discovered if I don't act fast, and well.

I pull away, say, "Mom, Ellie invited us to a party. Can we go?"

"What?" Mom says.

"A party. It's just for kids. Marky Barky said it would be okay." I've just made up that last part, of course. I have no idea what Marky Barky's position is on this. I've also made up that it's just for kids. Also that she's "invited" us rather than "coerced" us.

"Where is this event?" Mom asks. Her eyes seem like they are focused on something very far away while she's trying to look at me.

"I'm not sure. She's getting a PlaneCab," I say. "She said we have to go soon."

I'm concerned Mom will say no. But also hoping she will say no. She actually says, "Oh! My baby! Old enough to go in PlaneCabs with friends! I can still feel you and your brother nursing from me," Mom exclaims. She must have had a lot of Dog-quiris already. Maybe enough to make her not notice the whining noises emanating from my tote bag.

"We have to go," I say, kissing her cheek. "I love you." I hug her. I haven't hugged her in a long time.

"And I love *you*," Mom says. "My precious, beautiful daughter. My kitten." She then kisses Wolf and Jack as well. "You are all my children." She leans down to kiss my robot dog Billy on top of the head. He doesn't respond. "Take good care of them, good boy. I'm counting on you."

We walk away from the party, away from Mom, toward Ellie, and who knows what else.

Ellie's there, waiting, with the PlaneCab. It's fancy looking. Shiny black, about the size of a minivan. (Not that we have minivans on Dog Island, but I've *seen* them on television, you know.)

The door pops open.

"You brought the precious cargo?" she asks. I nod. "Well then get on in, you guys."

Wolf climbs in first. I wait a moment, I guess in case he starts screaming in fear or pain or something. When he doesn't, I get in next. Billy my robot dog follows, climbing up onto the soft seat next to me. It's like the inside of a limo—again, from what I've seen on TV.

Ellie is next, and then she goes to shut the door. But I lean out first.

"Jack?" I say. He's still standing there, holding his little robot dog.

"I can't leave my mom," he finally says. "I'm all she has." He is clutching Mr. Chi-Chi Pants.

"Okay, drama queen," Ellie says chirpily, pressing a button on a console. I watch Jack disappear behind the closing door.

As we take off, there's a barely perceptible hum. There are no windows, but the walls of this thing are translucent, so I see Dog Island getting smaller and smaller as we rise into the air and fly away, away, away, away.

Ellie is trying to make conversation, but I can't stop watching the scenery. The scattering of lights below us, the bodies of water you can just barely make out from this high up.

"This is your first time flying, I take it?" she asks me.

"Yeah," I say. "Wolf's, too."

Wolf smiles, puts his arm around me. Billy sits next to me. I take Donut out of the bag.

"May I?" Ellie asks. I hand him to her. She cuddles him, he nips at her. "Naughty," she says, in a soft voice. "Naughty puppy." How does she even know how to behave with him? I guess I sort of knew what to do, too, even though I've had no experience like this with the real dogs. The Organics.

Ellie's still chatting. She seems genuinely interested in us now that we are on her turf. "Do you guys go to school?" she asks. "I never understood what kids did at the sanctuary. Like, how did you learn anything?"

"We learned some stuff from people on Dog Island. We also had some Virtu-School when we could get the app to work. We don't really have Internet, though, so it doesn't work a lot."

"Oh yeah," she says. "I can see that. What about friends? Did you have friends? Did you go to birthday parties?"

"Yeah, sure," I say. I tell her we went, we go, to our parents' friends' birthday parties. We had, we have, each other.

"But who do you, like, make out with? Who do you lose your virginity to?"

My face burns. This is worse than the Bad Bitches at the Casino talking about me and Wolf getting married.

"No one," I tell Ellie. "I haven't lost my virginity to anyone." Wolf pulls away a little. We haven't quite gotten there, yet. Most of the Dog Island women who have sex with men get operations to install permanent birth control inside of them. I have not embarked on that path, as yet, and I don't really have access to other options. It would really be something to become the next woman in my family to have a baby as a teenager. No thank you.

"Oh ho, that's interesting," Ellie says. "I was only fourteen, myself. I was still acting then. He was in the movie with me. *Dance All Night*, it was called. They all thought I'd be another star! I got bored of it. You know that story, I'm sure."

"Of course," I say. I am so worried about saying the wrong thing. I wish I could be home with my friends and my robot dog and this puppy, and that nothing bad was happening.

Ellie opens a bottle of champagne. She hands me a glass, and one to Wolf.

"This will be good for you," she says.

"Getting drunk?"

"Seeing someplace else," she says. "Seeing a little bit of the world. C'mon kid. You must be curious what life is like outside of the island. Away from crazy Auntie Dorothy."

The truth is that I have never been curious about life outside of Dog Island. My life on Dog Island has fulfilled me. I have never needed more. I have never really thought about there being more. The champagne tastes sharp, like needles in my tongue.

"Why are we here, Ellie?" I ask her. "What do you want with us?"

"Be patient," she says. "And have some more champagne."

After about half an hour, the PlaneCab starts to descend. It's so smooth you wouldn't even notice, unless you were gazing out, watching the ground hurtling toward you. I brace myself for a crash, an impact that I know probably isn't coming.

We just glide to a stop in a stretch of grass, just outside an old wooden gate with ANIMAL KINGDOM written out in yellow block letters, alongside a huge carved elephant head. As we get out of the PlaneCab, I see a group of bright red birds swoop by, flying in formation. They fly right by us, then up over the gate.

"Those are still the original performing macaws," Ellie says. "Even though there isn't really anyone to perform for anymore. There's something so tragically beautiful about these birds still flying for an audience that no longer exists."

She's talking philosophy while I'm scared out of my mind and a little tipsy.

We follow Ellie past empty souvenir stands, ice cream shops ("shoppes") that have no ice cream, and motionless rides. The foliage is still thick and jungle-like. Somehow it survived through the dry years. I touch a leaf. Plastic.

We walk toward what sounds like loud cheering. We reach a cage that has a confusing and surely inaccurate sign out front reading WARNING: MOST DANGEROUS TIGERS.

"Come look," Ellie says. I push through a small circle of people to the bars and wish I hadn't. Oh my Dog, I wish I hadn't.

There are two robot dogs in the cage. One of them is biting and jumping and attacking, throwing the other one to the ground, over and over. Then that one gets up, runs at the attacker, bites the face, rips at the nose. People are cheering as one robot dog gains some ground, then the other wins an advantage, an eye is torn out, a tail broken, a leg bitten; they are both going to be decimated, ruined in there.

My robot dog Billy looks up at me, and I swear I see genuine fear in his lifeless eyes. Its lifeless eyes. What a trick. Is this Mechanical Tail's doing? Have they come that far—far enough to create artificial fear? Why would that be a desired feature?

"Why did you bring me here?" I cry out, squeezing my own eyes closed. "These dogs are going to die! How can you let this happen?"

"Don't be an idiot, Nano, they aren't going to die," I hear someone say. "They're robots."

I know that voice.

I open my eyes and see Billy. The real Billy. My brother.

We at Mechanical Tail have taken your input TO HEART. We HEARD you when you said that you were NOT HAPPY about your traded-in robot dogs being used for SPORT!

We LOVE that you LOVE your robot dogs. That's why we make them! To make you HAPPY!

We also want you to UNDERSTAND that it is environmentally UNFRIENDLY to simply KILL a robot dog. Do you want your robot dog in a landfill? NO!

So our pledge to YOU is that every robot dog you trade in will be RECYCLED and given a new life. Their parts, their programs, will become the FOUNDATION of a new robot dog. Isn't that MARVELOUS? You never have to worry again! Go ahead and trade up for one of our BRAND-NEW WATERPROOF ROBOT DOGS!

CHAPTER 7

Billy has changed. Of course he's changed. He looks older now. He has nice clothes. Fancy. Same as Ellie's kind of fanciness.

"Why do you look so fancy?" I demand of him.

Billy laughs. Odd, since I am not laughing or smiling or remotely happy.

"I missed you, kiddo," he says. He hugs me, long and tight. I don't want to hug him back but then I do anyway. "I've really, really missed you," he says. I think maybe he's talking to me and Donut both. Donut is squirming with happiness in my arms and licks Billy's face.

I shove myself away from him. His smile doesn't disappear.

"Hey man," Billy says to Wolf. He makes a fist and punches my boyfriend on the shoulder then resumes kissing and being kissed by Donut.

Ellie and my brother hustle us into a PlaneCab. I sit opposite Billy, staring at him. Ellie sits beside Billy, leaning into him. It's obvious that she and my brother know each other well. She tells me she's sorry she had to act like a brat on Dog Island to get me to come with her, but it wasn't safe to tell me the real reason I needed to go with her to Animal Kingdom.

I'd like to ask her more, about everything, but it's a short trip. We've reached our destination. There's a rocky thud as we settle on a flat surface. We clamber out. We're in a field. It's dark. My heart starts to pound.

"Welcome to Fuzzy Mansion," says my brother, spreading his arms wide, grinning broadly.

There are mounds of snow, and frozen grass, and leafless trees. Past some fences I see cows roaming. Turkeys, too, I think? Next to us there's an old wooden house, painted white; tendrils of smoke drift from the chimney. I am transfixed by the animals. Two fluffy, wooly sheep run up, accompanied by a goat whose hind legs are supported by a wheelchair.

"Hi Carol!" my brother says to the goat, who nibbles his jacket pockets. "Shalom! I've missed you, baby girl. Have you been good or baaa-d?" He looks up at me. "Get it? Baaa-d?" he repeats. "Because goats say baa? Oh, man, forget it."

I don't want to laugh, but I do. Mostly I want to punch Billy in the face. And hug him. I want to scream how much I've missed him, how I've hated him for making me miss him, how I want to cry. I am so cold and have so many questions, like *Where have you been, what happened to you, why did you leave, what are you doing here, do Mom and Dad know where you are, where did you get those nice clothes, what in the hell is going on here,* etc. etc. etc.

"Here, you must be freezing. Come with me," Billy says. It's the first thing he's said that seems to make sense. "I can't wait for you to meet Dave. And Hamlet! Especially Hamlet! I can't believe you're finally here!"

"Yes, and it will be nice for them to meet Fiona and Wanda, too," Ellie adds with a smirk.

Billy pushes open a heavy wood door. I step inside a cozy kitchen. The warmth and soft light wrap me up like a blanket. On a padded bench, underneath a row of windows, there's a rooster taking a nap snuggled next to a humongous pig. My brother introduces these two as Dave, the rooster, and Hamlet, the pig, all Organics.

I rush over to kiss and pet them. It gives me something to do besides piece together who my brother is or has become. On the other hand, it works. I can't hide my delight. Dave's feathers are very soft. He lifts one of his wings so that I can give him a good scratch. Not to be outdone, Hamlet shoves her head into my lap and insists that I rub her ears. I put Donut down on the floor so I can devote both hands to making these two animals happy. Dave coos and Hamlet grunts. Donut barks at us, then poops on the floor, then barks some more, wagging his tail the whole time. Wagging his tail, a little dog, in a home. This was once a thing that happened all the time; I know it was.

"Not what most people mean when they say they have a chicken and a ham in the kitchen, is it!" Billy crows. He eyes the poop on the floor then strides over to clean it up with a rag. He winks at Donut. "Thanks for your housewarming gift."

I finally summon the ability to speak. "What is this place?"

"A farm animal sanctuary," Billy says. "We take in injured

and unwanted farm animals. We give them a home here. By treating them well and sharing their lives, we show the world that pigs, chickens, turkeys, goats, cows, all of them, deserve our compassion."

I shake my head. *"We?"*

Before he can answer, a woman comes into the kitchen. She looks to be in her fifties, maybe, or perhaps even a little older. She wears a long loose dress with a turtleneck underneath and slippers with pig faces on them. She has long gray hair and her skin looks weathered. I've never seen someone so beautiful in all my life.

"This is Wanda," says Billy. "She's the caretaker. Of Fuzzy Mansion."

"Dog be with you," I say instinctively.

Her face flinches. "Hello to you, too. I see you've already met our spoiled kids here," she says.

My cheeks feel hot. I've displeased her, somehow. "You mean Dave and . . ." I can't remember the pig's name.

"Hammie," says Wanda. "We've had her going on a decade. She was just a wee piglet when she fell off a truck headed toward the slaughtering plant. A kind soul found her by the side of the road, nearly dead. Got her to us. It's a very different life we've managed to give her here, wouldn't you say?"

"I would say," I do say, rubbing Hamlet's big old head, thinking of the other piglets who must also have been on that truck.

A woman, a girl, maybe a few years older than me comes dashing into the room. "You're back!" she cries at Ellie, before throwing her arms around her and kissing her on the cheek, the neck, the ear.

"Hi, sweetie," Ellie says to the girl.

"This is Fiona," Wanda says to me, wryly. "My daughter. She's a senior in college and actually a very interesting person. But don't expect to find that out. You won't see a lot of her while Ellie is here. Ellie takes up all of her attention. Watch—Fiona, do you want a million dollars? Can I buy you a castle in France? See, nothing."

A little black-and-white cat with just one eye skulks around near the stove, in view but out of reach. Obviously, this is a real cat, not a robot. You can tell by the way the cat's tail twitches rapidly, swishing back and forth, before pausing in the shape of a question mark. Also, by having one eye and that eye looking Organic.

My robot dog Billy takes a clear interest. I nod "no" to him, so he won't grab the cat for me to examine. He looks annoyed. This amuses me, so I pull out my phone to press the "positive interaction" button.

Billy touches my arm. "Don't do that here. We aren't aiding Mechanical Tail. In helping to eradicate the world of living things or anything else."

"In what?" I say. If there were a "very freaking confused" app button, I'd be pressing it repeatedly.

"What *do* you actually do here?" Wolf asks. *He* looks profoundly uncomfortable. But still cute.

Wanda smiles. "We model compassion," she says.

"But what do you *do*?" Wolf asks again.

"I don't know how else to explain it," Wanda says. She

smiles warmly. "I hope you'll stick around a while and see for yourself."

"Wanda is being kind of coy with you because she's had some, well, extremely negative interactions with a couple of hard-core Dog Islanders in the past," Ellie says. "We rescue farm animals. The sick, the injured, the unwanted. The ones who are lucky enough to fall off a truck on the way to slaughter. We give them a home."

"Then," interjects Fiona, taking a break from slobbering all over Ellie's face and neck, "then we share their stories. Our aim of course is to make people love Hammie so much they want to make sure other pigs get treated well, too. We are very, very manipulative, when we get the opportunity!"

"You're part of this?" I say to Ellie.

"I give them money. So, so much money. I can't be more public yet because of my dad," she says. "One day. Hopefully soon." She smiles at Fiona. Fiona beams at her. I guess Ellie and my brother are definitely no longer a couple.

"Why would Dog Islanders not like this?" I ask.

"Right, exactly," Wanda responds, giving me literally zero insight into the issue.

I sit on the bench and lean back against the windows. The glass is cold against my arms. I wish Jack were here with us. It seems wrong for him to miss this. For us to be experiencing life without him.

I PrivateText him to see if he's okay.

He doesn't respond. It's late. He's probably asleep. Or at the Hot Bod after-party. Or hanging out somewhere with Mr.

Chi-Chi Pants, savoring their last hours, and mourning. Or he's angry with us for leaving.

I hold my phone in my lap for about a minute, trying to think of a follow-up text. Finally, I just send a heart symbol. I feel sad and guilty about Mr. Chi-Chi Pants but don't have the words to express it.

My lap is toasty warm where Hammie's heavy head rests. As is my side because Dave is snuggled against me. Donut lays at my feet, so my toes feel snuggly, too. Billy, my robot dog, sits near the stove, watching mechanically. Wolf and Billy—the real Billy, my robot's namesake, my brother—are deep in conversation with Wanda. Ellie and Fiona go disappear off to somewhere. I don't feel so angry anymore.

I like it here. I like it here. I am confused, and I like it here.

Wanda approaches me. She bends down so we are eye to eye. "You must be hungry," she says.

"Starved. I don't want to be any trouble though." It's got to be midnight or one, or Tuesday, or December. I don't remember if I ate dinner.

"We have some stew. It's venison," she says.

"Venison?"

"Deer. I hunt one deer at the start of every winter. We eat it the rest of the year," she says.

"Oh," I say. "I don't eat animals."

"Your brother didn't either when he got here," she says. "I get it."

"He does now?" I ask.

"Not much. He's not crazy about our other options either, though. He's sort of picky. It's a real pain in the ass."

I laugh in spite of myself and quickly bite my lip.

"Was he like that at home?" Wanda asks.

"Yeah," I say. "Always."

My stomach tightens as I picture Billy eating animals. This is part of an answer; this is part of the person my brother has become. This is not how we were raised. The Billy who was my brother at home would never eat a creature who'd had his or her life ripped away, violently. I guess in his old life, pre–Dog Island, this wouldn't have been strange. My brother had a life before me, and one after me. The expression on my face must give away my feelings because Wanda smiles sadly.

"You like Petunia?" she asks, pointing at the one-eyed cat still skulking around the room.

"Very much," I say. I'd run over to pet that cat if I weren't snuggling with a pig and a chicken.

"Petunia needs to eat animals in order to survive. She's what's called an 'obligate carnivore.' Do you know that term?"

I shake my head no.

"That means that Petunia will die if she doesn't eat animals."

"Oh. You mean like how the pelicans and herons have to eat fish?"

"Yeah. Like that," Wanda says. Her eyes brighten. "Pelicans. I love pelicans. We don't have a lot of those around here."

"We have tons of them on Dog Island," I say.

She nods. "I've been there, you know," she says. "Long time ago."

I instinctively look toward Donut, who has tucked himself

in for a nap near the stove. His white belly rises and falls. He twitches in his sleep. Petunia appears to be stalking him—she slinks up close and reaches her little paw, then pulls it back quickly when his eyes flutter open.

"We feed the dogs fake meat on Dog Island," I tell Wanda. "It's specially formulated."

"We might not have the right mixture to be able to do that here," she tells me.

"Is it hard killing a deer?" I ask.

"Hard?" she says. "I suppose. You're a hundred yards from a majestic living thing, knowing you'll be ending his or her life. My only other option is buying meat from someone else. I won't do that. Only eat animals that I or my family have killed ourselves. I use my grandfather's old gun."

I tear my eyes away from her. I look at the floor. "You don't seem surprised to see us. To see a real dog. Whose tail wags."

Wanda doesn't answer right away. Instead she kneels beside me. She rests her arm around my shoulder.

"We are very happy you're here, Nano," she says. "We've been hoping you'd come. I've been hoping that you'd come. Maybe even that you'd stay."

There's a long pause before I ask: "What's going to happen now?"

"I don't know, dear," she says. "Hopefully, something very good."

EVENTUALLY WE ALL SIT down to our late dinner. Billy has set the table, something he never did at home. Dave joins me on my chair, nestling behind me. Hamlet lies down next to the table, and I finally see how unbelievably gigantic she is. Stretched out, her body is as long as the table itself. Petunia hops onto my lap, curls up, and falls asleep. She purrs in her sleep.

Wolf makes sure to sit next to me, too. I'm grateful, but curious. How does he seem so relaxed and comfortable here? Is it a boy thing? Is he braver than I am? Or is it because he doesn't think too hard about anything? I can't imagine that his brain squirms with questions like mine. I imagine that his brain is just happy that his body will be fed. Maybe he'd act weirder if Billy were his brother.

The stew is doled out into bowls. Everyone eats it but me and Wolf. It smells really good, and I feel a little sick because of that. A big bowl is placed on the floor for Donut, who sucks the food down like it's the first and last meal he'll ever eat.

We eat the spicy eggplant and chard, and fresh-baked bread—the bread is so much chewier and richer than what we get from Dog Island Sourdough Vegan Bakers, and then I feel guilty for thinking that, and I think about Dad and how hard he works to keep us fed and how I have probably completely betrayed him and Mom and Dorothy and everything I know and love by being here at all. My brother, vegetable hater, declines the veggies here, too. That makes me feel a little better. My brother is still Billy.

When we finish eating, Billy invites me outside to help him feed the cows, and the turkeys, and the other pigs, and Carol the goat, before bed. Wanda starts clearing the table and washing dishes, using real water instead of a Dish Blower.

Wolf jumps up to help. An elephant-shaped vacuum cleaner travels the floor.

Wanda sees me noticing it all.

"Don't sweat it, honey," she says. "For the last couple of years we've started getting more rain and snow again. There's plenty to go around. We collect it and use it for washing dishes, flushing toilets, bathing."

"Can you drink it?" I ask, perhaps a little breathlessly.

Wanda pours then hands me a glass. It's delicious. Then she goes off to collect "more sensible clothes so you won't freeze your *tuchas* off."

When she leaves, Billy whispers to me that a *"tuchas"* is a butt, and Wanda is always extremely concerned about the condition of people's butts.

"That's . . . nice of her?" I say.

"Very," he agrees.

She returns with a set of clothes made of a thin, stretchy material that Wanda tells me will keep you "toasty when it's cold out and cool when it's hot. Like magic!"

I hear Billy telling Ellie and Fiona how much better Florida is than Maryland in "so many various and important ways, like the weather" while I slip myself into the clothes, in a drafty bathroom.

"Oh quiet," Ellie says to him.

"I speak nothin' but truth," Billy says in some kind of weird accent.

They talk like they've known each other for years. They have.

When I come out, Wanda helps me into a big thick coat,

and we walk out the door, accompanied by Ellie, Fiona, Hammie, Donut, and my robot dog Billy. (Petunia naps near the stove.) I note that the clothes really do the trick.

Ellie points to the PlaneCab still parked in the yard and says she's leaving to go back to New York. She says she'll be back tomorrow after class. She kisses my brother on the cheek, then me. She kisses Fiona on the lips, then walks off, with confidence. I can't tell if I like her as a person, but I think I admire her place in the world.

Fiona returns inside. My brother Billy and I make the rounds, feeding the dozen rescued cows, all who are living here after escaping their expected fate: the dinner plate. There are a few donkeys, some horses, more pigs. (Hammie seems to turn her huge, long nose up at them. Billy tells me that she's the queen of Fuzzy Mansion. She believes other pigs are beneath her, "and she's right.")

We visit with the turkeys. They live in a heated indoor-outdoor enclosure near the main house. They also seem very grumpy that their dinner is coming so late—nearly time for breakfast. Billy tells me his favorite part of every week is the Fuzzy Mansion turkey dinner, which sounds alarming for a moment, until Billy reassures me that it's when "we all cook up a big feast for them and us to share. They get to eat first."

"You like it here?" I ask him, while we make the rounds, accompanied by the animals and robot.

Billy says, "I finally feel at peace."

"What do you mean?" I ask him.

He shrugs. He doesn't look at peace right now. He looks annoyed that I asked the question.

When we go back into the house, Wolf takes me aside. "I got a PrivateText from Jack," he says. He shows it to me. It's Jack asking when we are coming home.

"Did you answer?" I ask him, feeling a little hurt that Jack reached out to Wolf but not to me.

"I said we'd be back eventually. We will, right?"

"Of course," I say.

Billy grabs my arm. "Come here."

I nod. It's a relief not to have to talk anymore about Jack, so I allow my brother to tug me into the living room. I find myself collapsing into an overstuffed couch, facing a crackling fire in the fireplace. It's so warm in here. A feeling of exhaustion suddenly overcomes me. It must be one, two, three in the morning now.

Billy hands me an old-school electronic tablet. As he withdraws, there's a snap of flame, a wisp of smoke. I see that he has a joint in his mouth. The sickly sweet smell of it fills the air. He sucks in and exhales.

"You can do that inside?" I ask, surprised.

"Wanda's an old hippie," he says, handing it to me. I shake my head. "She grows it here," he adds with a shrug, popping it back in his mouth.

He tells me to read the document he's opened.

Maybe I'm getting a contact high. I'm too drowsy and spent to protest.

CHAPTER 8

November 25: On deployment with WAG to The Fun Safari in Reston, VA, to investigate cruelty by dir. Megan Zilly. Xtreme Cruelty confirmed.

Donkey appears to have been axed into pieces. Sheep, 3, run over w/ truck. Wallaby dscvrd drownd and dead in bucket. Etc. Etc. Etc. 37 Dead in all.

7 srvivrs. Real bad shape. Skin & bones. Sick. No water 2 drink. Took pictures and videos to give to law enforcement for prosicution. Called Dorothy re: saving some. She said no. Fllowed protocol.

THERE ARE SOME MORE details, written in some more of Billy's Pidgin English—I guess the Virtu-School curriculum was worse when he was my age—along with the photos of the dead and the living.

I feel sick looking at them, more than reading the words. The twisted, mangled, worn-out, emaciated bodies of these precious creatures. I pull Donut off the floor and into my lap, and kiss each of his soft paws, his ears, his nose. He whines and complains.

I hand the tablet back to Billy.

"Why are you showing me this?" I ask him.

"Did you read it?" he says.

"You saw me," I say. "It was only a couple lines."

"Do you know what this means?"

"Some a-hole animal abuser got shut down but not soon enough," I say.

"Do you know what it means that I followed protocol?" he asks, slowly, carefully. Forcefully.

"You made sure no one else would suffer?" I say.

"It means I killed the survivors, Nano," he says. He looks down at his hands, then looks up again, right at me. "One by one, I followed protocol. Kinderend for all."

"You relieved their suffering," I say. I smile. We prevent suffering. That is what we do.

"Nano. These animals had been *tortured*. Somehow, they'd survived. And then I came along, like, in theory to rescue them. But all that meant was *death*. I could see in their eyes. They wanted to live, kid. I knew it was wrong, even as I was doing it. I felt I had no choice. This was my job. To make sure no animals would suffer. By *killing* them."

BILLY TELLS ME ABOUT administering what he thought would be the last dose of Kinderend that day. It was to an emaciated white bunny, missing big patches of fur, her skin raw and bloody.

As he made one more lap around this horrible roadside zoo, he saw Carol the goat. Rather, he saw her feet, her hooves, poking out of a decrepit shed.

He walked over, expecting to discover another dead animal. Instead, he found this young goat alive. Her back two legs—the ones sticking out of the shed—were mangled, he doesn't know how they got that way, just that she was badly injured. But her eyes were bright. She seemed to recognize him. She even lifted her head a little, though she must have been in tremendous pain.

Billy lay down on the feces-and-bug-covered floor and he stroked her head.

"Do you want me to end this for you?" he asked her, fingering the Kinderend.

She blinked, and smiled at him. He swore it was a smile. He cried, he tells me now. There was no going back. He knew, there was no going back.

Billy called Dorothy. He suggested with as much confidence as he could muster that Dog Island put some resources into an annex. It could be called Goat Island, for example. Dog Island II would also work. Dorothy's Magic Palace of Rescued Animals—that was also an option. The important thing was that it would house at least some of the animals Billy was rescuing.

He felt sure Dorothy would say yes. That she'd thank him for bringing him this good idea, this humane idea. She'd probably put him in charge of implementing it. Maybe Marky Barky would cough up the money. He tells me all of this, and it's clear it pains him, because he believed it.

"What did she say?" I whisper.

"She said no."

"Did she tell you why?" I ask.

He tells me that Dorothy said she'd "been down this road before" with the sanctuary in Texas, and it "doesn't end well." The animals were miserable. The inevitable bad *publicity* was miserable.

"We have the opportunity to offer these animals peace. Eternal peace. You want to deny them this for your own selfish reasons?" Dorothy said.

"So what did you do?" I ask, sensing that what he did was not good.

Billy tells me that he loaded the goat into his rental truck, then brought her to a veterinarian whose clinic he'd spotted on his way to the zoo. The vet's name was Dr. Samira King. Dr. King asked Billy how the goat had gotten so hurt, why he'd waited so long to take her for care. Billy said it wasn't his goat. He'd just stumbled on her accidentally, he said. There was no one around, and he couldn't bear her pain.

"She should probably be euthanized," Dr. King said. "She won't ever walk again."

"Please, save her," Billy had pleaded. He tells me he felt like his own life was dependent on this one. ("I felt like I was going to die if she died," he says.)

The vet agreed to do what she could, but couldn't promise much. The goat was very sick and very injured. The goat's back legs, which had stuck out from the shed, were beyond repair and had to be amputated right away. Then it was a matter of IVs, antibiotics, careful monitoring, and waiting, for a couple of weeks at the animal hospital.

Billy, of course, had no money to pay for this treatment (a fact he conveniently hid from the vet, at first). When she learned of his poverty, Dr. King suggested Billy reach out to Wanda at Fuzzy Mansion. She told him she'd worked on some of their animals before. That they were "extremely compassionate if somewhat kooky people, who would sacrifice everything for the sake of helping animals."

Wanda was more than glad to hear from Billy. She gave him enough money to pay the vet bills. They had a custom wheelchair specially made for Carol, and when Carol was stable enough to leave the hospital, she was brought to Maryland and given another chance.

"You could call it a second chance," Billy tells me Wanda told him. "This was really her first chance."

Billy stayed a little while at Fuzzy Mansion while Carol got situated. He found, there—here—a sort of peace and purpose he hadn't known before.

When he came home to Dog Island, he couldn't help thinking about what he'd seen there. It was different from our home. It wouldn't have been fair to call it *better*, he thought. It was different.

"I just didn't know that it was even possible to save them," he tells me. "I feel so dumb now for that. I just didn't know."

Billy tells me he couldn't stop thinking about Carol. He couldn't stop thinking about the other Fun Safari animals whose lives he'd extinguished. Out of kindness and because he'd been ordered to do it. But why couldn't they have lived, too?

"I mean, it was really flipping *unbearable* once I started thinking about it," Billy tells me.

Billy made an appointment to see Dorothy. She had him over to her house, a Spanish-style home on a small hill overlooking the water. They drank tea and ate sugar cookies from Dog Island Sourdough Vegan Bakers. Billy felt nervous, he tells me, but also certain. He said to Dorothy he thought Dog Island should open an ancillary sanctuary, or series of sanctuaries, where the animals We Are Guardians rescued could live.

"What about the exotic Organics?" Dorothy asked. She meant animals like lions and cougars; idiots would buy them from breeders and then try to keep them at their houses. (They used to do this with tigers, too, until the extinction.) It is so cheap to buy a lion now that someone who can't afford meat or water can get one, then ruin it. Lions may start off small and docile but quickly grow large and ravenous. Their stupid owners end up locking them in basements, tying them to trees, and not providing them with enough meat and water to thrive since the drought had driven up prices for both. So when WAG gets called in, either by the owners themselves or by concerned neighbors, the animals are dehydrated, starved and miserable, sick and dangerous. And there's no obvious safe and healthy place for them to go after their rescue.

As I listen to Billy, I understand. *There are fates worse than death.*

"I told her we could build a sanctuary for them," Billy says. "She asked me if I knew how many lions are in captivity in the United States alone. I really had no freaking idea. I guessed maybe a couple hundred. But I was wrong. Dorothy said there were five thousand of them, 'at least.'" He makes air quotes. "Then she gave me her spiel about how they are 'mostly in really rotten circumstances.' She asked me where they would go, once we got them out. How we could keep them happy and safe. They need a lot of space. What we were going to feed them. I guess the food would be really expensive. And they would have to eat a lot. So there's that, too."

"What else?"

"She told me: 'Billy, there's unfortunately only one right thing to do. You know what it is. Don't become one of those crybabies who can't handle reality. Now scram. I have work to do. We all have work to do. Aren't you going off to North Carolina today, to that chicken farm?'"

So he left.

That night he went on a WAG deployment to a chicken farm where 15,000 chickens had been left in a barn when the area flooded. These chickens were bioengineered in such a way that even during the best of circumstances, their lives were "totally impossibly grim," as Billy puts it. They'd been bred to have breasts that would have been comically large if they weren't so cruel and needlessly tragic, the deformity leaving them unbalanced, unable to walk, unable even to lie down comfortably. And these weren't the best of circumstances.

Before the flood, the chickens were packed into tight cages, stacked up on top of each other in a windowless barn.

Their lives had "literally no pleasure," he says. "No sunshine, no fresh air, no good food, no toys, no comfort."

These animals' whole purpose was to grow meat and then die so that those humans who haven't switched over to lab-grown or other alternatives could stuff themselves with their carcasses.

Billy opens up his tablet again. Shows me the documentation: *thsnds chickens ded in flood. Drownd trapped in cages. PU*—he tells me this is the code for "smelly." He holds his nose with his thumb and index finger to illustrate the point. Then he shows me the photos. They make me want to puke. The birds trapped in their cages, bloated like balloons. I can't even imagine their fear and pain as the water rose, knowing they were trapped. Billy says he wore a gas mask, and even that couldn't cover the rancid, evil stench of all those drowned birds as he trudged over the muddy dirt floor, picking through the wreckage, to find any survivors.

Miraculously a few survived. He wasn't sure how they made it.

Billy was going to give them the Kinderend in the barn. Then he thought it would be better for them to die outside, with fresh air. Let their last moments be pleasant.

One at a time, Billy carried these birds outside. They had filthy white feathers, cloudy eyes, sores. Their beaks and spirits were broken. Their huge breasts heaved, as they tried to breathe. Billy felt broken, too, sitting with them on the muddy ground. They tried so hard to get up, and walk, to flap their wings. They made pathetic "cheep cheep" sounds, looking at him.

Billy took off his gas mask. He wanted to show the chickens a friendly human face. He doubted they'd ever seen one. "Be pacified. Be loved. I bring you peace and happiness. Let's proceed," Billy tells me he said, tearing up as he says the words. "Then I couldn't do it, Nano."

He tells me he thought about calling Dorothy again. He tells me he felt so tired. His head was all buzzy. And without really thinking things through, he put the birds in his truck and began to drive north. He knew the truck had a GPS device, it's not like he could hide where he was going, so he didn't alter what would have been his regular route—just thought he'd run into a vet's office, here in farm country, at some point. But he didn't. So he searched on his phone. One clinic came up, a half an hour away. It was arguably in the right direction. He called to see if they were open and could see the chickens.

"No, sorry, we don't do birds." Billy imitates the voice on the phone in a whiny singsong. He tells me he wanted to punch her in the face.

He called Dr. King. She told him to come in; she'd stay open for him, for them. It took almost three hours to get there. The whole drive, he kept telling the chickens: "C'mon, guys, or girls, or both. You can do it. Stay strong, mother cluckers."

He was aware of the absurdity. There in a truck, telling a few near-dead, preposterously large-breasted chickens to be strong while he raced them to a far-away hospital, against Dorothy's orders.

"It was so *ridiculous*," he says to me.

He kept driving.

Two of the chickens died en route. At the end of the drive, one was still gasping, fighting to live. Dr. King fixed this one up, too. This chicken stayed living with Dr. King. She said she saw her as a "fluffy little symbol of hope and redemption" who is "also incredibly cute." Billy smiles, giving me Dr. King's sweet words.

She named the chicken Boobie McChicken. Billy laughs when he tells me the name. "Boobie McChicken," then informs me that Dr. King "isn't married but has a stupid boyfriend."

After that Billy came home again.

He relaxed for a couple of days. Swam, kayaked, helped feed the dogs. Hung out a lot with a college girl who was there doing a semester-long internship. They smoked ample amounts of weed. Then Dorothy called him back to her house.

No cookies and tea this time.

Dorothy asked him to look out before him, at the beach, the Casino, the blue sky, the Ruffuge's outline just visible from where they stood.

"You like this, right?" she'd said to him. "Dog Island, which I built to provide a safe home for the world's remaining dogs and the people who love them?"

He told her he loved it. Even though in his heart, he was feeling increasing doubt.

She said, "I will make you leave this community forever if you ever pull a stunt like that again. I will kick you out. Your parents. Your sister, too. I will make sure all your lives are ruined, forever. And I will kill one of the dogs, too, in your name, for your betrayal. Do you understand me?"

Billy didn't *really* understand. But he also did.

He was taken off the We Are Guardians team, permanently. Reassigned to the Dog Island maintenance squad. Garbage collection, painting, lawn care, fixing broken toilets, all over the community. He was devastated in some ways; in others, it was a relief. At least for a little while. Just a little while.

One day he was in Patricia's house—one of the Bad Bitches—unclogging her kitchen sink. He was telling her she had to stop trying to stuff bread and Ethical Chicken into the garbage disposal. He was in the middle of his lecture about how not to royally freak up your plumbing when she interrupted.

"I hear you and Dorothy had words."

He said, "Not really," because there was no need to get the rumor mill going.

But Patricia said to him, "You aren't alone in this." Then she thanked him for fixing the sink. He says that people repeated the same thing in other houses—that he wasn't alone—and before he knew it he realized that there was a *group* who all spoke in this same code, who all had this same understanding. A mission.

It took a couple of weeks before he learned what this group was calling itself.

"THE 'UNDERDOG TAILROAD,'" HE says to me now. "I don't think it's the best name," he clarifies. "But they are real attached to it."

I nod. "It's not . . . great. Maybe a little confusing and also kind of offensive."

I have one hand on my robot dog Billy who's next to me on the couch; the other on Donut, asleep in my lap, while my brother Billy paces in front of us, oblivious—or maybe just stoned.

"You can tell who was a part of it, by looking at everyone's lawn flamingos," he says.

"The pink plastic ones that are everywhere?"

"Yeah," my brother tells me. "But if someone's in the Underground Tailroad, the flamingos' eyes are different. They look up instead of straight out. That's the code. Took me a while to get it, but then I started seeing those flamingos all over the damn place. At the Bad Bitches' homes; Marjorie's little bungalow. Wolf's parents. Jack's mom. Maybe half the houses on Dog Island. Half of the houses were apparently on board."

"Was ours?" I ask hopefully.

Billy shakes his head. No, not ours.

"So then what happened?" I ask.

He smiles and sits beside me. "It's late. There's so much for you to see, kiddo. We'll go on a little trip tomorrow."

"Okay," I agree reluctantly. I feel disloyal now. And homesick. "Mom and Dad must be worried. I should call. Let them know I'm okay. Maybe I can tell them I'm with you?"

He stares at me. His lips quiver. "Not yet, Nano," he whispers. His voice is strained. "Give it a little time."

I give it to him. I am so tired.

It is finally time for bed. Wanda, wearing a long plaid flannel nightgown, offers Wolf a guest room on the first floor. She gives me flannel pajamas of my own and puts me to bed in a small bedroom on the second floor, with a window that overlooks the cow pasture, and a tall bed covered in quilts.

Donut and my robot dog Billy come up to sleep with me. They rest next to each other at my feet. Hammie comes up to my room, too, but Wanda calls her away, saying I'll have no room for myself if she hops up there with me, too.

Wolf comes up to join me, sometime later. He climbs into bed with me. We touch and kiss. He produces a pill from his pocket that Ellie gave him. She told him it does something to the sperm so they can't fertilize an egg. That sounds like a useful little pill, I tell him. He says he likes my flannel. It feels soft, he says. It feels like a dream.

FRIENDS: We are going to lay things out for you as clearly and truly as we can. Serving your companion animal needs by creating the World's Best and Most Realistic Robot Dogs has been a DREAM come TRUE.

But now we need your help. We endeavor to make every robot dog your BEST companion and friend. We work with the Good People of DOG ISLAND to get every detail exactly RIGHT.

The feedback we get is VERY GOOD. You LOVE your robot dogs. We LOVE that you LOVE your robot dogs. You love them so much you are not participating in our buyback program. We were too good at our job!

Unfortunately, due to declining sales, Mechanical Tail has been forced to close 75 percent of our showrooms and to retire our entire mobile showroom fleet. We will maintain an online presence, which we hope will continue to serve your ROBOT DOG NEEDS.

Please tell your FRIENDS and FAMILY to purchase ROBOT DOGS from our ONLINE STORE, so that we can continue to provide the VERY BEST ALL-ETHICAL COMPANION ROBOT ANIMALS to you.

CHAPTER 9

I wake up the next morning to Donut licking my face, nibbling my nose. Who could have ever dreamed that a real puppy could be snuffling all over my face inside a house like this?

After a while, I get up and look out the window. The whole property is covered in white.

I smile, my nose pressed against the icy glass. I *do* like it here.

DOWNSTAIRS WANDA HAS FIXED a big breakfast with real coffee. I sit down at the table. Wolf is already there.

"Shalom, good morning!" I say to her. Wolf grins, probably at how chipper I sound. I can't help it. I am practically bouncing out of my seat. I'm excited to be here with Wolf, to go feed the animals again, to tromp around in this exotic weather, to learn about this strange place and these people. But Billy tells me to go get dressed for our "field trip."

"Did you *sleep* well?" Ellie asks, sweeping into the room. She fixes Wolf and me with a smile and arches her eyebrow. Her tone is snarky for someone wearing a bathrobe and fuzzy slippers. Of course, she has the supreme confidence to make even *that* look cool.

I blush. "Yes, thank you."

After a spell of eating and eating and eating more—pancakes, coffee, eggs from the resident chickens—I eat these, even though usually eggs are forbidden. It would be rude not to. I cannot believe how rich they taste. Usually I get droopy when I eat too much, but the coffee is so dark and tasty and *powerful.* Woo! I could eat all day, I think, but Billy says it's time to go out.

I get a shower, a real shower, with water and soap and a soft towel. Wanda gives me a new set of clothes for today's trip. Not that I know from clothes, but the pants, sweater, boots, and coat look upscale. Ellie does my hair and puts some makeup on my face. I look sophisticated! I feel my bearing change, after seeing myself like this. I have a feeling of what it might be like to be a normal adult on the mainland, who, like, has a job in an office. (Maybe Wolf and Jack work there, too?) I have a feeling that I would not like that life for very long but for now it's okay.

ANOTHER NEW EXPERIENCE: RIDING in a real car. Billy, Wolf, robot dog Billy, and I pile into a huge luxurious vehicle that is kind of like a living room on wheels, with a television for us to watch. Billy, Wolf, robot dog Billy, and I pile into a huge luxurious vehicle that is kind of like a living room on wheels, with a TV and everything. It's so smooth, unlike the GoPad; the Auto-Drive never jerks to a stop or suddenly speeds up without warning, like a person. It's a cold, clear day, but the big clear bubble on top lets in the sunshine.

Wolf and I sit facing Billy. We hold hands. Wolf seems to have a little light in his eyes. Maybe he feels closer to me now. Or likes me dressed up like this. Does he like makeup? I suddenly feel self-conscious.

"So this is new," Billy says in a loud voice.

That snaps me out of my reverie. Wolf drops my hand, and I see that my brother is looking us both up and down. He slouches back in the upholstery.

"What are you talking about?" I ask him.

"You two," he says, nodding his head at us. "A couple. A *thing*. Two Organics in the thrust of youth."

My face is suddenly hot. But I only shrug, squeeze Wolf's hand. Impulsively I kiss his cheek. He responds by kissing my lips. I am back in my Wolfish trance. My makeup and hair are probably being destroyed but . . .

"You know, you could pretend like you care I'm right here," Billy says grumpily.

AFTER A LONG TRIP along many winding roads, the car takes a right onto a long driveway. Billy pulls a bag from under his seat. He dumps it out on the floor between us: they're what look like costume props. He affixes a fake mustache onto his own face. I stifle a giggle. After attempting to put a thinner, blonder mustache on Wolf, he rips it off, muttering something about "looking like a teenage perv." He puts a baseball cap on Wolf's head instead.

We gently glide to a stop in front of a new-looking large brick house. It seems out of place in these surroundings. Mustached-Billy and Wolf-in-his-cap and I get out of the car, leaving my robot dog behind.

"Follow my lead," my brother says under his breath.

He rings a doorbell. A friendly looking man with a beard answers. He looks pleased to see us.

"Aiden!" the man says. "How the hell are you?"

"Terrific, Cody. Couldn't be better," Billy aka Aiden replies.

I get it. We're undercover. He could have told us as much on the trip.

Billy waves his hand at us. "I want you to meet my friend Ashley and her brother Fred."

Ashley? Wolf is my brother? I try not to grimace.

"Hi Fred," Cody says, holding out his hand. Wolf shakes it with vigor.

He doesn't shake my hand and barely even seems to realize I'm here except for looking me up and down once, slowly. I've heard lectures about "nasty sexists" from Dorothy plenty of times, so I recognize what this is. It's almost exciting meeting a real-life sexist in the wild.

"So, what are you kids in the market for?" Cody asks.

Billy (as Aiden) answers on my behalf. "They are new to the Organic live experience. Just taking a look, so they can begin considering their options."

"Cool, cool. There's always a first time," the guy says. "Well, come with me."

I restrain myself from holding Wolf's hand as we follow him through a gaudy home. It's dark inside; there's a lot of heavy wood furniture with metal accents, like whoever decorated it wanted it to seem like a medieval castle. There's nothing on the walls other than weird gold-framed family photographs of what I assume are a dozen-odd grandkids. Maybe they're just stock photos. Who has that many blond relatives?

At the end of a long hall, we enter a living room, where a large pen holds five puppies. They are golden-colored, soft and small, and romping around one on top of another. They pay us no mind whatsoever. No growls or barks, but also no wags.

I hear Wolf's phone buzz. He's gotten another PrivateText. His face sours when he glances at the screen, but he quickly replies. Billy shoots Wolf an irritated look.

"They're real?" I ask. I feel a physical urge to touch the puppies. It's taking all my willpower not to run to them.

"One hundred percent," says Cody. "Bred them myself."

"How?" I ask.

"As God intended," he replies. "A male and a female. You need me to explain the birds and the bees, chicky?"

I feel myself blushing. "That's not what I meant."

"She's curious about their lineage," says Billy, glaring at me over his stupid mustache. "You understand: there are a lot of bones on the table here. Let Ashley and Fred meet the parents, so they can see they're healthy and strong. You want their money or not, man?"

Cody grumbles but finally agrees. We walk to a less gaudily appointed part of the house. He opens a locked door, turns on a low light, and we walk down some stairs. A sharp stench burns my nose and throat. That's nothing compared to the

sight that greets us: four small wire cages, with dogs inside—
one small black dog, one small tan one, two big yellow dogs.
I'm horrified. These dogs look just like some of the current
lot at the Ruffuge. Except these are filthy and look sad and
are confined so tightly they can't move. They don't make a
peep at our arrival. I'm too stunned to speak, either.

"See, healthy," Cody says. "The pups are third generation captive, so they won't complain about being in a cage.
We can breed yours in a year and share the profits. You
have to be very discreet. No one can know you have them.
Do you have your basement or shed prepared to house
one of these puppies? If not I can recommend a guy who
does excellent work. Your neighbors won't hear a peep,
will never know you've got one of these dogs, so long as
you follow my rules."

I am about to explode. I am about to say something I
shouldn't. Something to Cody. Something like: *You are an evil
monster. You are inflicting suffering on these beautiful creatures. You
should be locked in a cage like this. You should be forced to sit in your
own filth, with no hope of escape. You should be so lucky to have Kinderend offered to you. And you, Billy, how could you take me here?
How could you show me this horrible thing?*

Instead I say, "Let's go back upstairs."

My brother sneaks me a grateful look. We return to the
puppy room. After a deep breath, I remember that I am
"Ashley," a despicable person. I ask Cody if I can pick one of
the puppies up. He says no, that it's not safe for me to be with
them, nor safe for their future owners.

"They get your scent in them, then you belong to them

and they belong to you," he says. "You won't change their minds. They won't imprint on whoever will end up with them. If you want to put down a deposit now, then you can touch the one you're going to buy, but I'd prefer you not."

Billy nods quickly, stepping in front of me. "She's just getting a feel for the market now. Not ready to make a deposit," he says. "But if you're looking to off-load any of those breeders I can take them off your hands. If any of 'em are done pushing out puppies, we can use them as target practice. I know some folks who'd pay big bucks for the chance to hunt a real Organic dog."

"Nah." Cody shakes his head. "Not yet. I'll call you when this crop's about through so we can make plans. Might not be for another year."

"Okay, brother," says Billy, steering Wolf and me toward the hall that leads back to the front door. "I'll be in touch soon."

Cody follows us through the darkened halls. I don't realize my own mouth is hanging open until I see that Wolf's is, too. Then all of a sudden I'm squinting in bright sunshine and a blast of freezing cold wind; I shiver and run for the car.

Back inside, Billy the robot dog hops up and wags his tail jerkily. As soon as we slam the door, I lean down and hug him tightly. Wolf and Billy stare out the window, watching Cody watching us.

"Keep it together until we are out of sight," my brother mutters.

Somehow, somehow, somehow, I do.

"YOU OKAY?" BILLY ASKS once we're out on the main road. He's pulled off his mustache, at least. Wolf's hat is still on his head. I touch it and he looks at me, his eyes sad.

"What was that hellhole?" I shout at my brother. "Why did they have dogs? *How* did they have dogs? Why don't we stop them? I have Kinderend. I stole it from Mom before I left. We could have done it right then."

Billy doesn't answer right away. His eyes are on the bubble overhead. "I know," he says finally. "It's awful. I was real shook up the first time I saw one of these breeders."

My stomach lurches. "*One* of these breeders?"

"There's about a dozen that we know about."

"We? You mean Wanda and Fiona and Ellie?"

"Yeah, and everyone else." Billy sighs. "I almost forgot how totally shocking this is at first. Until I saw your face, and his."

He shoots a glance at Wolf.

Wolf looks ashen. He asks to pull over. Billy presses some buttons, and the car rolls to stop by the side of the road.

Wolf gets out and vomits. I jump out to follow, but Billy grabs my arm. Wolf smells bad when he re-enters the car, but I take his hand. He pulls it away. He won't look at me.

"You okay?" I whisper.

"He'll be fine," Billy answers for Wolf.

I glare at him. For some reason, my brother then decides that this is the perfect time to repeat the entire story he told me last night. At least he's not stoned, so it goes fast. Wolf just nods, nods, nods. Mostly he looks like he wants Billy to shut up. I also want him to shut up, especially when he begins to explain that the Underground Tailroad operated without much of a plan.

"See, we were desperate to get some of the puppies and dogs out," he's saying. "You know, before they were killed. So we didn't spend enough time thinking about where these animals would end up. It had to be somewhere secret. Ellie with her money and connections and persuasive abilities—they placed the animals with some guy named Dom. He told her he had a remote piece of property in southern Virginia where as many as fifty dogs could be kept safely, happily, until more permanent plans were made. Or they could stay there forever, he said. Dom just wanted to help."

I hold my breath, sneaking glances at Wolf. The color is returning to his cheeks. I'm so busy trying to figure out if he's okay I don't even notice when he reaches for my hand and takes it, not until my fingers are intertwined in his.

After that, Billy's rambling doesn't seem so bad. Or at least not as bad as before.

Billy goes on about how Underdog Tailroad members needed help. They were so ecstatic to have a safe haven for their at-risk dogs that they didn't ask enough questions. They became emboldened. Their animals were sedated and packed into cages, transported to Virginia, where Dom apparently made a big deal about how happy he was, participating in this noble act. He made a big deal about how he was blessed with enough money and space to make sure these precious animals would always be taken care of.

And then one day—about a year and a half ago—an Underdog Tailroad smuggler arrived to find Dom's property shuttered and the dogs gone.

It took a few months to find out what had happened to them.

Dom had sold the dogs to exotic animal collectors and breeders. Not run-of-the-mill monkey and lion peddlers, gross but mostly legal. No, these are people who operated in an extremely secretive fashion, selling animals that aren't legal to be bought, sold, owned, or hunted. The most valuable obviously were dogs, real dogs. Organics. By now they've been bred, who knows how many times already. Organics can breed twice a year; they can give birth to as many as ten or fifteen puppies at a time.

Some of the Underdog Tailroad wanted to search for all the dogs and puppies, to track them down, to give every single one a Kinderend. Others wanted to quit for good. Others did quit, in their own way. One felt so guilty she gave herself a Kinderend.

"Was that Belinda?" Wolf asks suddenly, interrupting Billy's monologue.

"Pardon?"

"The one who . . . ?"

Billy nods.

I nod, too. I remember going to her funeral. We had a service for her at the Dog Island Chapel then a big picnic at the beach, even though it was really hot out.

"I didn't know that's how she died," Wolf says. "Or why."

Billy's face hardens. "It was wicked bad. We pretty much shut down then. But Ellie and I wanted to make things right. We had a plan, even. Ellie would use her contacts and connections, and money, to try to track down and get back as many of the dogs as possible. I introduced Ellie to Wanda. She promised to donate money, so much money, to Fuzzy Mansion, too—"

"You felt guilty," Wolf snaps.

Billy says, "I couldn't leave Dog Island to go looking for the dogs because Dorothy was still keeping me off WAG. There was one thing I *could* do, though. I signed up for as many feeding shifts at the Ruffuge as I could get. I volunteered extra hours, to fix fences, and cull back weeds. I was determined to spend all my time around the dogs. So I could get to know them as individuals and have them learn the same about me."

"Why?" I ask.

"We domesticated dogs," Billy says simply. "People, I mean. Human beings. Or we used to. For as long as we've had human civilization. And they domesticated *us*. We've been joined for so long, us and them, I just had a feeling we could be like that again," he says. "That we could stop the killing. Like, for real."

"Donut," I say.

Billy tries to smile. "Donut," he echoes. "I spent so much time in the Ruffuge. I was so happy. Happier than I'd ever been, surrounded by six wild, dangerous dogs throwing themselves at me to get me to play with them. I mean it. They trusted me. Either we were going to make this work or they were going to kill me, and either one was okay with me honestly, Nano."

I think of Donut, chewing on my hair, tussling around me, cuddling up close and snoring. His sweet breath, his damp snout, his wrinkly skin. The improbability of his existence.

My robot dog Billy looks at me, sticks his nose under my arm. I put my arm around it. Around him. He leans against me, closes his eyes, as if he is napping.

THE UPSHOT IS THIS: Billy took a leap of faith—a giant leap, but a mistake.

One day, almost exactly a year ago, he asked Dorothy to come with him into the Ruffuge. He wanted to show her how the dogs were behaving; not viciously, not violently, but like they were his friends. As if they enjoyed his company. As if they were redomesticating. Because if they weren't dangerous anymore, if they once again wanted to be with the humans, didn't that mean that things could start going back to how they used to be? Wasn't that proof we should end the killing?

Dorothy agreed. He'd never felt such relief or joy.

The dogs seemed happy to see him, as always. They approached, sniffed, wagged their tails. They did not do the same with Dorothy. At her, they lunged, teeth bared. One jumped at her. Another tore at her dog suit, ripping off a piece of fabric on her butt. Billy would have laughed a little if they'd done that with anyone else. With Dorothy, he knew there would be bad consequences.

"I'm glad you brought me here," she said, after they'd left. "Now I know what your project has been and that it is a failure. If I can't trust my own people to behave morally maybe I should just shut down Dog Island right now. End this enterprise. Chalk it up as a failed experiment. It's so small, anyway. So very small in the grand scheme of things. My larger goal is to end all suffering. This place is a tiny speck of dirt to be scrubbed clean."

"What do you mean, end all suffering?" Billy tells me he asked.

"Foxes eat birds, birds eat fish, fish eat other fish. The world is terrifying and full of pain . . . I want to make that pain go away. Robots," she said, declining to further explain.

Billy went home that night and tried to talk Mom and Dad into leaving Dog Island. He confessed to them what he'd done. He told them about Dorothy's plans, insofar as he understood them—which he didn't, really; he just knew she had something dastardly and bad in her head. He told them about her not-super-veiled threat.

"Oh honey," Mom told him. "Just be a good boy. Can't you just be a good boy? Honey, sweetie, dear boy, this is our *home.*"

So he decided to disappear.

THE CAR IS SILENT for a while. But I can't stand it anymore. I muster the courage to tell him what I really think, how I really feel. Wolf's hand in mine helps; his grip grows stronger.

"You just left me," I say, feeling upset and not completely rational but also not totally un-rational. "You left me, not knowing what would happen. I could have been killed. I could have *helped* you. Why didn't you tell me?"

"I didn't just leave you," he says. "I came back to give you the dog suit. I knew I could trust you to carry on my work. And now, look, here you are."

Then my robot dog Billy opens his mouth.

"Please call, Nano, kitten, my love," he says in Mom's voice, but a quavering version of that voice. "I don't want to scare you. But we are all in trouble. Please, just call. Please, Nano."

Wolf says quietly that that's what his PrivateText said, too. The one he got back at that horrible breeder's house. It was from Jack. He said things were getting bad.

"When I asked him what he meant he didn't respond," Wolf says. "I'm really worried."

With that, the gravity of all we've done and seen hits me.

"What should I do?" I ask Billy, my brother.

"Ditch the robot, first off," he says.

I hug Billy my robot dog closer. "I can't," I say.

"Nano, don't be an idiot. They are obviously using it to get to you," he says. "It's not *real.* It's a robot."

"Please, no," I beg. "How can they use him to get to me? He's just my robot dog. You know he has GPS and you let me bring him anyway. That can't be the issue." It occurs to me that I am probably hurting my case, not helping it.

"Nano, through this hunk of metal, they can *reach* you. One word from Mom through that stupid robot and you are ready to leave and go back home. We have too much work to do for that to happen."

"Why did you let me bring him with me at all?" I ask.

"I have my reasons," Billy says. Then he looks ashamed. "I just felt badly saying it had to go. I don't know, kiddo. I could see that you're starting to love it . . . I didn't want to hurt you. Again."

Billy is right. After hearing Mom's voice I just want to go home.

"Let's get back to Fuzzy Mansion," I tell my brother.

My robot dog licks my cheek with its synthetic tongue.

My brother Billy stops the car.

He opens up the pod, gets out and places robot Billy by the side of the road, then gets back in.

As we drive off, I stare out the bubble to watch my robot dog Billy getting smaller and smaller. He, it, sits there, watching us go.

REMEMBER how the scientists really screwed up? REMEMBER how all of our beloved dogs got sick, thanks to them? REMEMBER how our beloved dogs succumbed to genetic experiments and un-Organic viruses cooked up in a lab?

REMEMBER how they stopped wagging their tails?

That was BAD science. BAD science made Organic Dogs dangerous, too dangerous for this earth.

Robot dogs are GOOD science. You missed the dogs so much when they were gone. WE MISSED THEM, TOO. That's why we created MECHANICAL TAIL, DAMMIT! So that we could be with dogs again.

And we help FUND Dog Island, so that the world's last dogs will be safe! Does that really not MATTER to you anymore? What can we do to get you to buy our robot dogs again? Please, nothing sick or illegal. That is NOT what we are creating these robot dogs for and we do not want to hear from those disgusting people PLEASE. Our lawyers are on call.

CHAPTER 10

"Mom tried to reach me. Through my robot dog Billy," I say quietly to Wanda in the kitchen. It smells good. Wanda and/or Fiona are always making good things to eat. Wolf goes into his room to be alone. I feel a lump in my throat. "It's gone now."

Wanda nods calmly. "What did she say?" she asks.

I'm trying really, really hard not to get emotional. "She asked me to call. She said she was in trouble."

"That's good news," Wanda says.

"It is?"

"Oh, for sure," she says. "Look, because of your brave brother here, Dorothy knows that there are . . . dissenters. She doesn't know how many or what they are capable of. But now she knows that you've left, that you're with Billy. She must have some idea that Ellie has joined our side. She's probably freaking out." Wanda waves her arms around and shakes her head, saying these words; it seems perhaps a little more exuberant than the situation calls for if you ask me.

I shake my head. "How is that good?"

"Because it means she's either going to negotiate, or she's

going to behave rashly. Either way, we can finally expose her for who she truly is. Someone who hates animals. And people. Someone who wants to kill everything. The leader of a death cult. *Then* we can liberate the dogs and stop her from harming other animals as well."

"Death cult," I repeat. I roll the words around in my head. They don't make sense. "We save the dogs on Dog Island," I hear myself say. "How is that a death cult?"

"You save a half dozen at a time, while killing anything else you can get your hands on." This from Fiona, who appears at Wanda's side. Her face is colder and icier, like the air outside; she uses the word "you" like a whip. She doesn't know anything about my home, yet she feels free to say these hideous things.

"*I* didn't," I reply after a moment, testily.

"I didn't mean you personally," she mutters, turning away.

"How do you know Dorothy's going to do something extreme?" I ask Wanda.

"She's said she would. If Dog Island were ever endangered, she would kill everything and everyone there preemptively. So the Organics wouldn't 'suffer.'" Wanda makes air quotes with her fingers, again giving the impression of being happier about all this than I feel is correct.

"What do you think she means by that?" I ask.

Wanda stares at me. "It's in her will."

I shake my head, at a loss.

Wanda's pretty, wise eyes narrow to slits. "You never saw her will?" she asks, incredulously.

I didn't even know that Dorothy had a will or that anyone

would have seen it. Why would I? What on earth does that have to do with *me*? I've never heard of any of this before. My own parents have never talked about a will. None of the rest of this sounds right.

Wanda gets up from the table and follows Fiona out of the kitchen. I'm by myself for an excruciating minute or two until Wanda returns alone with some sheets of paper. I am shocked but also curious as she hands them to me. Printed paper and sexists and meat eaters . . . all of these things still exist. She must see my wide eyes; she shrugs.

"Screens hurt my eyes," she says.

I stare down at the words.

DIRECTIONS FOR THE DISPOSITION OF DOROTHY BLODGETT'S BODY

I skim the dense and baffling legal language. But I get the gist: in the event of her death, Dorothy wants her body to be used by Dog Islanders in all sorts of ways—ways that are equally incomprehensible.

The "delicious flesh" of her body is to be cooked into a stew, divided up equally among all the human residents of Dog Island, and consumed at her wake. Her skin is to be treated as leather and turned into shoes for Dog Islanders to wear, so she will always be with us as we "walk the path of righteousness." She wants her head to be mounted onto a piece of wood and hung in a special memorial, "alongside the other animals who have also suffered and died for our amusement and pleasure."

The worst comes at the end.

Any and all dogs still living at the time of my death should be released from suffering, as I do not trust any human in this cruel world to ensure their safety. Any Dog Islander who wishes to join our dogs and me in the Afterlife shall be granted this same option. If Dog Island is jeopardized, this option will be encouraged. We are one with the Universe. We go in peace and love.

"How did you know about this?" I whisper, looking up. The papers rustle; my hands are trembling. I put the papers down and go to lift Dave into my arms. We sit at the bench by the window, the cool glass on my back. Dave coos and purrs softly, which I appreciate. Donut appears from wherever he has been sleeping or hiding or getting up to mischief and yips at Dave. Dave remains, literally, unruffled.

"I thought everyone knew," Wanda says with a sigh. She is wearing her pig slippers again. They are so whimsical; the opposite of this conversation. "Dorothy had some kind of a press conference about it a couple of years ago. Everyone wrote her off as an eccentric, except the true believers. If anything, it enhanced Dorothy's standing and power." She takes the papers from my hands and offers a sad smile. "Go figure."

Moments later Wolf walks into the kitchen. I can tell he was lying down; he has creases on his cheek, and his curly hair is askew. The sun is shining through a window, and I can see the rings of gold around his hazel irises. I pat the seat next to me, signaling him to sit.

Instead he deliberately walks to the other side of the room and crosses his arms.

He's glowering. I don't understand this. I feel sick inside.

My whole life has likely been . . . not what I thought. In a really bad, bad way. Dorothy wants us to *eat* her. My family has been complicit in killing, rather than saving. Or both. We've done both. And I loved it. I loved Dog Island. I loved my life there. I would give anything to go back and not know what I have learned. I would give anything to go back to the way Wolf and I were before any of this—when we were a "thing," as Billy said. Are we not anymore? Did I do something? Did Billy tell him something?

I'm about to blurt out and ask Wolf what's wrong when Ellie walks in through the front door. She shakes off the cold and glances at Wanda.

"Where are we?" she demands. "Is the plan in place? Dad just left after his long naked visit with Dorothy, which I don't really understand." She cringes. "Really, for sixteen thousand reasons. But he's out of harm's way now and we can get going."

I cringe, too. And bristle. How dare she sound so casual, so ready to make decisions for us, about us. Unable to stand Wolf's glare, I stare down into Dave's feathers. Donut is so excited about his friend returning that he races around the room, squawking and wagging his tail, wagging his tail, wagging his tail, wagging his tail. This tiny miracle would be dead back home. Back home is home. Back home is where we protect the dogs. Back home is where Dorothy is going to destroy everyone and everything I care about.

"So what is the plan?" I ask.

CHAPTER 11

Fiona lays it out. It's pretty easy and maybe anticlimactic, even. She wants to stream a video with me and Wolf, and Donut and Ellie. Ellie will then introduce us as "refugees from Dorothy's death cult." We're supposed to say that we barely escaped with our lives. ("The truth, from a certain point of view," according to Fiona.) Ellie will then call for Dorothy to peaceably hand over Dog Island and its inhabitants—canine and human and everyone else— to an outside party, which will dedicate itself to life instead of death.

Dorothy must also abdicate responsibility over any other animals. She must stop trying to convince people that it would be better for Organic cats to be rounded up and killed and replaced with robots, for example. Etcetera.

"Do you really think she'll do it?" I ask when they've finished. "Dorothy, I mean. Do you think she'll go along with what you're asking for? You've read the will, too, right? And you're grown-ups. What do *you* think?"

I want Wolf to jump up, rush to my side, defend me. He doesn't. I look at the faces around the room—the other faces, the faces of these women, these strangers, my brother—and I can't quite read their expressions.

Finally, finally, finally Wolf speaks to me. "No, Nano. She won't go along with it. That's not what these people are actually after."

Not what I was hoping for.

"Is he right?" I ask Billy.

"Kiddo, we're at the endgame of a long battle," he answers.

"I don't know what that means," I respond, feeling panicky. I have a creeping sense that Wolf knows way more than I know, and maybe he has all along. "What does that mean, exactly?"

"It means that there may be casualties," Wanda says.

"Can anyone here speak English?" My voice rises. "What does this *mean*?"

Wanda sighs. "We wanted to shield you from the ugly part of this," she says. "You've already gone through so much."

"Why are we being so coy?" Billy says, sounding anguished and frustrated. "Just *let's tell them*. Let them make actual decisions for once in their lives. They live as if they are robot dogs. They've been preprogrammed in every way. We all were. Let them choose now." It hurts, and rings true, to hear my brother say this.

"Okay," Fiona says. "Okay. The video will do one of two things. It will either draw Dorothy to Fuzzy Mansion for a negotiation, which may or may not be fruitful for both parties. This will allow Dorothy to save face and preserve some power, for example, while limiting her ability to do harm—"

"You know what the second thing is, Nano?" Wolf shouts, interrupting her. "Fiona doesn't want to say it, but the second thing is that Dorothy will do what she promised and kill everyone and everything. And then you will have proof that she was as bad as you say. And you'll win. Which is what you really care about."

My jaw drops. I shake my head. That can't be right.

Billy says, "We hope that won't happen."

"So you've heard this, and we're good?" Ellie says. "We'll make the video? I can reach out to all my contacts and tell them to watch in an hour. It's settled?"

Wolf pushes away from the table with a loud screech of the chair. "Nothing is settled," he snaps. "I want nothing to do with any of this."

He looks at me. I've never seen him look like this before—furious and beaten. But I also see that I was wrong. He was never upset with me. He was upset that I was dragged into this. He was upset on my behalf, upset that he might have played a role.

"We need you," Fiona says, softly, her voice pleading.

"No," Wolf says. He looks at my brother Billy. "Don't you have any loyalty?"

Before Billy can answer, Wolf storms out of the room and runs upstairs, I guess to my room. I flinch when I hear the door slam.

Ellie shrugs. "Well, two is really redundant anyway. One of you Dog Islanders will be enough. Let me think about wardrobe . . . Maybe a long floral dress? No, that's too 'polygamous in the desert.' Hm. What did you wear here? That weird silver thing? I guess that might work? You wouldn't really *wear* that dress if you weren't trapped in a death cult . . ."

I am struck by a number of horrors, among them the prospect of appearing to the world as a crazy person in that *dress*. But I have an idea. Or the idea behind an idea.

"Let me talk to Wolf." I stand up and back away from the table. "Let me try to convince him. Give me until tomorrow. Okay?"

More inscrutable glances, more heavy silence.

"Please?" I beg.

Fiona nods.

I am not relieved at all. I am scared. I don't know if it will be enough time.

ONCE NIGHT FALLS, I accompany Billy as he makes his rounds and feeds the Fuzzy Mansion animals. Hammie and Donut and Carol are in tow. They play and run and sniff and explore so happily, so innocently. (Well, except Donut, who keeps trying to bite Carol's wheelchair, and wags his tail vehemently while doing so.) I wish there were a way we could just stay here—Wolf, Billy, and me—and get rid of *them*. I wish we didn't have to *do* anything.

I've wished that before. It seems that it's not to be.

Late in the evening, everyone goes to bed. I go into my room and huddle under the covers to stay warm. Wolf has long since left the room; he disappeared before sunset. Last I saw him, he was sleeping on the couch in front of the fireplace. He won't be back.

Hammie isn't sleeping with me tonight, either. She's off with Ellie and Fiona, I think. Donut is here, lying on my chest, nibbling on my fingers. He has sharp little teeth and sweet breath, and a wrinkly face. I look at him, trying to take in every detail. If nothing else, we let him live, for a while. Happily, safely, with love. And we got to see proof that this is possible.

I pick him up and kiss him on his head, his belly, his back, his paws, his long ears, his nose. Then I get out of bed, dressed in some summer pants and a shirt that I found in one of the closets, and carry my puppy down to Wolf.

Wolf is still asleep, though the fire has burned down to glowing embers. Even asleep, his face looks worried. His lovely, lovely, lovely face.

I wake him up by kissing his forehead. His long lashes flutter open.

"Hey, oh hey," he says, groggily. Then he remembers that he's angry or wants to be. "Leave me alone," he says.

"I'm not one of them," I say back.

He sits up, looking at me with more sympathy and interest.

"You know that. Being mad at me won't help."

He blinks a few more times. His beautiful eyes are glistening. He nods.

"We have to go," I tell him.

"Where?" His voice is thick.

"Home," I say.

Without asking more, Wolf nods and stands. I watch as he methodically puts on his clothes. Together we head outside into the bitter cold. Straight to the PlaneCab. Such a decisive act. At the PlaneCab, the plan stalls. We're suddenly stymied.

It's wholly unclear how to get this vehicle to take us where we need to go.

I remember there being a console or something? I'm not sure how it's involved, though, and now I can't even figure out how to open the door. Brave, ignorant girl, I am. I thought saving the world, or at least my little corner of it, would be more action and less searching for a way to open the door to a confounding PlaneCab.

While Wolf and I examine every mysteriously unyielding inch of the PlaneCab, my brother Billy appears.

"Hey. Can I help you with something?" he asks. His voice is dry.

"Billy," I say. "I have to go back."

"I wish you wouldn't."

"I know," I say. "You could come."

"I can't," he says.

Before I have time to worry about him turning us in, thwarting our scheme, he reaches in and pushes some magical spot on the PlaneCab door. It opens. With some other quick maneuvers, the thing whirs to life.

"It's all set. Get in," he says.

My throat is tight. I am on the verge of crying. I can't say the words, so I hug him. This is goodbye. I've missed him so much and will miss him again. I take that canister of Kinderend I've been toting around out of my bag and hand it to Billy. Just in case he needs it for anything. Even at Fuzzy Mansion, Organics will get sick, they will get old. Eventually, it will be time to help them pass. Just, only after they've really had the chance to live.

Billy turns around and walks back into the house before the PlaneCab takes off. I sit on the plush seat, looking outside. Donut is in my lap. I take Wolf's hand. He doesn't. He holds my hand back.

I squeeze my eyes closed as the PlaneCab takes to the air. When I open them again, I see my robot dog Billy sitting across from me. Billy is crouching down low by the wall, as if it is trying to hide. Billy blends so well, in the dark cabin, so as to barely be seen. Billy's head hangs, but I can see the eyes peeping up, looking at me. Eyes that are so like the robot cats'—bright, electric.

He found me.

"Come here, Billy," I say, patting my knee. He lifts his head. Rises to his feet. That's when I notice that one of his front legs has been torn in half. His tail is snapped at its base. The "fur" has been partly torn from his face. Someone has cut off his nose and one of his ears—the one that used to hang down. He has big holes in his "skin" and "fur." The shiny, blinky electronics beneath are clearly visible. He shoves his head into my lap, under Donut, and I pet him.

Wolf clutches my hand harder then goes to pet Billy but Billy isn't interested. He just wants me. He's been programmed for it, but it's okay. I understand.

It seems to take much longer to get back to Dog Island than it did in the other direction. Wolf and I don't talk much during the trip. We don't mess around, make out, tell stories. We don't even really talk about going home. Eventually he naps, leaning on my shoulder. He and Donut both snore a little. My heart is full, for them.

Billy and I stay up. He's awake because he's a robot, and I'm awake because I don't really know what I'm getting into. I just know I have to go home.

IT IS STILL DARK as the PlaneCab descends over our palm trees, our brightly colored houses, our neat brick streets. I can see the big silhouette of the Casino coming into view, the beach-side, and The Smiling Manatee just across the street. The Ruffuge over there is just a mass of thick plants. You can't see the dogs from up here.

We land nearby to where we'd taken off—how many days ago now? I can't even remember. One or two I think. So much has happened and changed that it feels like a month, a year, a whole lifetime. It's all a blur now. The PlaneCab door opens, and Wolf and I, and Billy and Donut, walk out. It's hot outside, already, this early in the day.

I wasn't exactly expecting to be greeted by a marching band. Still, I was half expecting Jack to meet us. It's weird no one is around. Wolf and I look at each other as we walk the empty streets. I notice the houses with the flamingos on their lawn. In the last moments of darkness, I can't tell which ones have eyes that are looking up.

Wolf and I stop at the beach for a few minutes. We stand, his arm around my shoulder, mine around his waist, looking out at that beautiful water as the sun starts to rise. Donut runs around in the sand, yipping and making mad dashes. Give him this moment of freedom, I think, while we know he can have it. My robot dog Billy sits at my feet, looking up at me, while I watch the sunrise. It is a bright orange and pink and yellow, filling the sky. I've loved it here. My whole life I've loved it here. That is not a lie. Even if everything else is lies, that is the truth.

I pull out my cell phone, unroll the flexible screen, and am about to push "positive interaction" out of habit, out of love. Then I don't. I guess that part of things is over.

I point to a nearby palm tree. "Palm trees aren't actually trees, you know. They are grasses. If you cut them down and count their rings, you will not see how long they have been alive," I say. "Though that is true for many of our plants because the drought really screwed things up as far as botany goes."

"I didn't know that," Wolf says. "Thank you for sharing this important new information."

I smile at him. I kiss him. "You're welcome," I say. I don't think we will have too little to talk about for a while to come. Still, I like our old standbys.

We get going again before the sun is fully up. There is a lot to do today. I pick up Donut and hand him to Wolf. He whines and wiggles. I kiss his head and nose. Lifting him, I can feel that he's already gotten bigger. He is less the size of a donut and more the size of a very small loaf of bread.

Maybe I'll change his name to Small Bread Loaf, if we make it through this.

Please, dear Dog, let us make it through this.

I tell Wolf to hide and not to tell me where he's going. There are caves, abandoned buildings, he knows every spot where nobody goes. I don't want to be able to tell

Dorothy where he and Donut are, in case she wants to do something bad.

"Just make sure he's safe," I say, trying very hard to feel brave.

"Make sure *you're* safe," Wolf says.

He kisses me. Leans his forehead against mine.

"Bye, Nano," he says, walking away.

I turn the other way to head for home. I want to talk to Mom and Dad before anyone else. Now that the sun is up, people are starting to appear. I walk briskly. Marjorie rides by on her bike, with Harold on her shoulder. She is in a fluorescent-bright caftan, and rings her handlebar bell, and calls out, "Shalom and peace be with you, Nano!"

Harold chimes in as well, "Shalom! Shalom! Peace! Shalom!"

I turn to watch them; her hair and his feathers both fly out behind them.

Luckily nobody else seems to notice me. Maybe that's why when I get to the house, I am feeling more confident, more optimistic.

I PrivateText Jack to see if he is there, if he needs help.

He doesn't respond. Maybe he's still asleep. Or maybe who knows what. I head into the kitchen and find Dad, his back to me at the stove, cooking up breakfast. He looks the same, which surprises me. But I haven't been gone long, even though it feels like a lifetime. I sniff the air. Smells like pancakes and that vegan sausage he's always saying, unconvincingly, doesn't taste like garbage.

There's even a whiff of coffee. I can't remember the last

time we had real coffee instead of getting caffeine in pill form.

"Hi Dad," I say to him.

He whirls around, startled. "Kitten. You came back." His voice is a whisper. He drops the spatula and rushes over to hug me. As he kisses the top of my head, he breathes in my ear. "You shouldn't have."

CHAPTER 12

Dad makes me a plate of food. It is, of course, not very good but I gobble it down. We eat it quietly for a little while. I explain to Dad about being at Fuzzy Mansion. About how the people there called Dog Island a "death cult" and are now trying to get Dorothy to kill all our dogs. So they can prove to the world that she is bad, her ideas are bad, that dogs belong with people, that the world's animals shouldn't be exterminated and replaced with robots.

It all sounds so insane, coming out of my mouth.

I decide to conclude with a question. "Dad, are they right about Dorothy?"

He shakes his head. "We didn't know it would get like this," he says, still whispering. "We were just kids ourselves when we got here . . ."

Then it all comes pouring out of *him.* How Dorothy recruited Billy onto WAG, so that he could become one of her chief assistants and advisors, so he could see how much cruelty there still was in the world, even with the dogs having been saved. She thought he'd help her execute her bigger ambitions. Billy didn't see things her way, of course. And when Billy and Dorothy first started tangling, Dad advised Billy to stop. To get along. To "go with the flow" since Dorothy was and is our leader and she knows what's best, and this is where we *live*.

Billy failed to take this advice. Things came to a head. Billy had to leave.

Yes, Dad was desperately sad. So was Mom. They tried to look at it as a choice. Billy would go off into the world and have an adventure. That's what you should do in your twenties. The rest of us would stay here. That's what you do when you are not in your twenties. That was what was best for the family.

According to you, I think.

Dad looks so miserable. He *should* look this miserable. He brought us to this place. He did this to us. Mom, too.

I rest my head in my arms. It's all real. It's all real.

After a few minutes of this, I lift my head.

"Where is Mom?" I ask.

"I don't know," he says, returning to the stove.

For all I know he's lying. He's clearly much better at lying than I ever imagined.

WHEN DAD GETS THE call from Dorothy, as I knew he would, it's time to go. My robot dog Billy and I are leaving Dad at home. I wish he'd come with me, with us. Of course, Dorothy was quite insistent that I come alone.

"You don't have to," Dad says, tearing up.

But he's wrong. I do. Of course I do. It's about a mile to Dorothy's house. I try to savor the walk, the beautiful morning.

We're there in no time, though—back at that familiar two-story Spanish-style, newly painted, like all our homes. She has such lovely landscaping out front—some palms, some flowering bushes, some cacti, and a water fountain. It spews recycled piss.

I knock on the heavy wooden door. No answer. I push it open and go into her cool, lovely foyer. She has such gorgeous things. Old rugs, rustic-looking wooden furniture, smooth and shiny with use. Expensive—all donated by her supporters. The paintings, of dogs and extinct species, don't quite match, but still seem right. I walk through the reddish kitchen, with its big old stove. There's a silver tea kettle, as always, sitting on one of the burners. I've had so many cups of tea in my life, made using that kettle, hanging out at Dorothy's house with Mom and Dad.

"Shalom, out here, dear," I hear Dorothy call.

She's outside on the balcony, sitting at her little tiled table for two, drinking tea and eating a small bowl of something very brown that looks exceptionally horrible.

Mom is sitting there, too.

So maybe Dad *was* telling the truth when he said he didn't know where she was. Or maybe not. Mom looks like she hasn't slept in a week. She tries to smile. I run to her to hug her. She clutches me like a life raft.

Dorothy wrinkles her nose. "When you get to be my age, you'll see how hard it is to keep your figure," she says. "When you're young, all you have to do is throw on a T-shirt and show up. My age, you have to make an effort. Your body doesn't want to cooperate. It wants to hold on to every calorie, every wrinkle. Being vain isn't easy!"

She takes another bite and then pushes aside the bowl.

Mom and I are silent.

"Be a darling," Dorothy says to me. "Fetch me a donut off the counter. There's a box of them. You can bring out the whole thing. We'll all eat them together. And then you will keep on being young and gorgeous and your elderly mother and I will have to do Jazzercise for three hours just to fit into our pants."

I look at Mom to see how to gauge all this. She won't meet my gaze.

So I go into the kitchen and put the donuts, six of them, on one of Dorothy's heavy earthenware dinner plates. Each donut has an approximation of Marky Barky's face on it, done up in icing. These must be leftovers from the VIP brunch that Dorothy hosts on the morning after the Marky Barky banquet. Here they ate donuts with Hot Bod while there I learned about cruelty and lies. I use a knife to cut each donut in half.

Dorothy notices my handiwork and raises an eyebrow. She picks up a donut half and bites into it. "Ooh, heavenly. The Dog Island Sourdough Vegan Bakers have really outdone themselves this time. Ruby, you eat one, too," she says to my mother. Then she pushes the plate toward me. "You, too, kid. We need to get some flesh on those bones.

What can I do? I eat a donut. I think of Donut. I wonder if there is a message in this food choice. I look out at the view. It's very pretty. Getting sunny and bright. I wish I could sit on my mommy's lap. Her head is fully turned away from me and Dorothy now. She is just looking out at the sea. I've never seen Mom this quiet.

Enough. I clear my throat. It sounds phony. I don't care. "Dorothy, I heard some terrible things."

"I'm sure you did, sweetheart," she says breezily. "They're out to get me. They're out to get *us*. They have been for a very long time. They don't believe in our way of life. They think animals are ours to do what we will with. Not that we owe them a duty to protect them from harm. Isn't that right, Ruby?"

"Yes, of course it is," Mom says.

It sounds so reasonable. Almost. "Isn't death harm?"

Dorothy smiles and lifts her shoulders slightly. "I suppose in a way it is. I don't like to think of it that way, though. Death is inevitable. Whether we hasten it or not, whether we like it or not, it's coming. So if we can see a life will be full of hurt and pain between now and that end, why not provide relief? Would you want to be in pain, to be mistreated? To be tortured? Wouldn't you rather just go to the eternal peaceful sleep?"

My mind is getting muddled again. I thought I knew what was right. I thought I had to convince Dorothy or defeat her. "I saw another way, Dorothy. It was so beautiful. There was a goat in a wheelchair and a six-hundred-pound pet pig named Hammie—"

"Child," she interrupts. "Those people you were with. They don't love animals like we do. They *eat* them. They think it's proper for animals to be *used*, for our enjoyment, our entertainment, our food. You know better than that! Tell her, Ruby. Tell her she knows better than that."

"Please, honey," Mom says. "Kitten. Please."

"But what about Carol?" I ask.

"Who, child?" Dorothy says.

"The goat. The one in the wheelchair. The one Billy rescued, even though you told him not to. She's so happy. She loves her life. Don't you think she deserves to love her life? You really think she should be dead?"

Dorothy looks amused. "I didn't know Billy had given this poor goat a name. Can you imagine her suffering? And now we keep her alive, to make *us* feel better." Her face softens. "Nano, we do our best, with limited resources, with limited information. You saw a puppy mill, I am given to understand. Do you think that's better than what we have here? This paradise, for the lucky? Should the unlucky be condemned to that hell? Wouldn't it be better for them not to exist at all? What do you think, Ruby?"

"You're right, of course, Dorothy," Mom says, still staring over the water, looking like she is going to faint. "Dog knows, there are fates worse than death."

I look down at Billy, my robot dog, who is so battered. Who found me, after I abandoned him. If he were real, Organic, he'd be dead, too.

"You know they want to stop you," I tell her. "They're trying to get Dog Island shut down."

"Every great movement has its enemies," Dorothy says, nibbling on the confectionary Marky Barky's face. "I can't believe you're letting me eat so many of these vile pastries. Here, hand me another."

"Do you think it's going to work?" I ask.

She looks right into my eyes. It's unnerving. She's so confident. "What do *you* think?" she says.

"I don't really know," I say, as boldly as I can muster. "I came to see if we can figure something out together. To compromise."

Dorothy's eyes darken. "It would be wonderful, fantastic, to live in a utopia where we could be assured that they would be safe. We don't live in a utopia. I will never back down when it comes to doing what is right. Never. I thought I could count on you to do the same. You were the one I had my eye on, Nano. All along. I thought one day you would take over here. Once this old body of mine gave out. Or my mind. Whichever came first."

I shudder. And feel proud. Dorothy believed in me.

"Well, let's stop stalling," Dorothy adds with a sigh. "Be a love and clean this up while I get dressed, will you Nano?"

Unable to speak, I obey. I bring the tea mugs and plates back into the kitchen. I remember my device and conquer my fear enough to PrivateText Jack again. Still no response. No indication he's even read my messages. There are a couple of donut halves left. I put them back into the box and load the plates and mugs into the Dish Blower. I wipe my hands on my pants then kneel down to pet Billy. I tug on his remaining ear and kiss the side of his face.

"I hope I can get you fixed up soon, my friend," I tell him.

His tail wags and thumps on the floor, very lightly.

SHE MUST NOTICE ME staring at her head.

"Yes, okay, you caught me. Old Auntie Dorothy sometimes takes real showers instead of using those disgusting wipes.

So sue me. You want a shower before we go? I've got fluffy towels, too, but don't tell anyone."

In a way, I'd like to take Dorothy up on this offer. I imagine fine-smelling soaps; I imagine coming out renewed. I imagine putting off whatever is coming next. But what is coming next is important.

"Later?" I ask, hopefully.

She smiles. "Okay, well, then, let's get this show on the road."

She and I, and Mom, and my robot dog, tool around town in her private GoPod. It is a mess, strewn with detritus—crumbs, wrappers, some mysterious liquids. I sit in the front passenger seat. Mom and Billy sit in back. Dorothy chatters, and the rest of us are silent.

Our first stop is Marjorie's house. I notice flamingos on the lawn. Their eyes are looking up. I breathe in, deeply. Dorothy knocks on the front door and Marjorie answers, in that bright caftan I saw her in this morning. Harold is on her shoulder.

"Good morning," says Harold. "Who's a good bird today?"

"You are, my sweet," Marjorie says back to him. She steps aside to let us in.

"How are you feeling? I know you were a little under the weather," Dorothy says.

"Oh, just getting older, mostly," Marjorie responds. She pats her hair.

"I've been concerned about you, Miss M!" Dorothy says. "And your feathery friend here."

My heart stops.

"No, no, no. Don't worry about us," Marjorie says with a nervous laugh.

"Well, I am. I know you were out of commission a few days here," Dorothy says, in a gentle tone of voice. She walks into Marjorie's living room, which is done up in a cheerful red and orange and green and blue and yellow parrot theme, and sits on a wicker chair that is upholstered in vintage parrot-print fabric.

"Come join me," Dorothy says, patting the couch, next to the chair.

Marjorie is trembling as she sits down. Harold climbs down off her shoulders and onto her forearm. She strokes his feathers. He makes a pleased, rumbly noise, while she does it.

"I think it's gotten to be time," Dorothy says. "And I think you know that, too."

"I don't . . . I'm sure I don't know what you mean," Marjorie stammers.

"Marjorie, when you were ill last week, you were unable to properly care for Harold. I know this. You know this. There's no succession plan in place. You are the one who has rejected every person who's offered to take charge of Harold's well-being, in the event that you're no longer able to do so. You don't want him to suffer, do you, Marjorie?"

Tears are rolling down Marjorie's face. They are falling onto Harold's beautiful feathers. He seems to be aware that something is wrong. He lifts his beak and rubs it against Marjorie's hand. Dorothy holds out her own gnarled palm. Mom removes a small container of Kinderend from her plain tote bag. She hands it to Dorothy, who hands it to Marjorie.

"I assume you will want to be the one to give Harold this peaceful transition," Dorothy says.

Marjorie takes the canister from her.

"I'll take him," I say. "Please, Marjorie, Dorothy. Let me do it. Marjorie, you'd be okay with that?" She says yes. So does Harold.

Dorothy sits back for a moment, as if she is considering this proposition. Then she says, slowly, "No, I don't think that is the best plan."

Sobbing, Marjorie begins to chant: "Be pacified. Be loved. I bring you peace and happiness. Let's proceed." Dorothy and Mom chant with her, as she says it three times, then opens the canister. She kisses Harold, while holding the Kinderend to his face. In seconds, he is dead. His wings hang limp. His beak is slightly opened. Marjorie cradles him like a baby. She begs him to come back to her.

Dorothy says, "You've done what's right and humane and necessary. Now he will not suffer, and your loyalties have been proven. Bring his body to the Dog Island Chapel. He can be part of our community forever."

DOROTHY AND MOM, AND my robot dog and I get back into the GoPod. I can't stop shaking. But Mom and Dorothy are acting like nothing unusual just happened.

"Why did you do that?" I finally ask, after a couple of minutes.

"I won't compromise," she says. "When it comes to doing what is right."

"How was that right?" I cry.

"It is selfish to want an animal's companionship, more than you care about the animal's suffering," she says.

"He wasn't suffering!"

"Stop it, Nano," Mom warns. "Stop it now."

Dorothy waves for her to relax. "No, it's okay. It's good to restate our values from time to time, at crucial moments."

Then she asks Mom to pass the dog suits from the back of the GoPod. Dorothy tells me to put mine on while we're driving. It takes some maneuvering, but I get it on. It fits better than the last one I'd worn. My brother Billy's dog suit. I stare out the window as we drive. My robot dog Billy climbs from the back seat into my lap. I wrap my arms around him and hold him close to me.

Funny: I wish Mom would speak to me through him right now.

Dorothy drives us to the gate of the Ruffuge. I go inside the guard house to ask for the gate to be opened. George isn't on duty today. It's Jack's mom, Betsy. I hug her; I wasn't expecting to see her.

"Please save him," she whispers to me.

"Oh no. No. Jack," I say.

She nods, looking terrified.

"I'll do anything it takes," I promise her, trying to sound as if that is something I am in a real position to promise.

I go back to the GoPod. The gate opens. We drive into the holding pen. The second gate opens, and we enter the Ruffuge.

WE DRIVE FOR A while and then stop. I'm not sure why, or where. I think this is the part of the Ruffuge where we found Donut.

As I'm getting out, Dorothy hands me a canister of Kinderend. She doesn't explain herself.

We walk a little bit, my robot dog next to me on one side. Mom is on the other. She takes my hand. Our paws, clasped. It's so quiet. I hear a few howls here and there, a couple of yips, but it's unnervingly quiet.

I see a little bit of motion up ahead. Hear some rustling. A howl that's somewhat louder. We walk closer. Fear turns to terror. Soon we're pushing through a thicket of bushes and trees. They are catching my dog suit, tearing at it, trying to stop me from moving. I get through. What I see on the other side is a nightmare.

About a hundred feet away, I see Jack. He is in a dog suit, with the mask removed. His hair is still crispy. His hands are tied behind his back.

Two other people wearing dog suits stand by him, I suppose to ward dogs away.

I don't recognize them by their shape and size. Normal grown-up sized. They could be anyone. I drop Mom's hand and start to run toward Jack.

Dorothy shouts, "Halt!"

I stop in my tracks. One of the people in dog suits pulls out a knife.

"NO!" I yell, but Mom comes up to me, puts her hand on my shoulder. She shakes her head. The ears on her dog mask jiggle back and forth.

"How can you let this happen?" I whisper. She shakes her head again. I can't see her face but I swear I can tell she's crying.

Dorothy says, "Go on," and the person with the knife

begins to cut Jack's dog suit away. The arms, the legs, a slice from the middle. He is only wearing underpants underneath. Dog-print boxer shorts. I want so badly to cover him up, and take him home, and get away. But I just watch. My legs are frozen in place. When the material is mostly gone, I watch in horror while one of the dog-suited people holds Jack, and the other inflicts gashes on his skin. A long one on each of his arms, a circle on his belly, small stabs on his legs.

He cries out as it is happening.

I do, too.

"Nano?" Dorothy calls. "In a moment your mother and I will leave. The dogs will soon arrive. Only five of them now. I had to give one a Kinderend yesterday. She hurt her paw, got a little cut, and I couldn't let her suffer. These five, they'll smell the blood. The human blood. Your friend Jack's blood. And, then—I really hate putting it like this, but let's be factual. They will try to eat him. Rip his *flesh* from his bones. I assume you will be okay with this, since it's not any different from your friends at Fuzzy Mansion eating meat. I know you believe that they have all the answers."

I refuse to turn around. My eyes are on Jack's.

"You can stay," Dorothy continues. "You can watch if you want. You can even try to help. I gave you that one can of Kinderend. You can try to use it on the dogs but I don't see how that's going to be possible. You could also use it on Jack, I suppose. Make this easier for him. Of course I will be forced to tell the public at large that we had a 'tragic incident' which led to all the dogs having to be euthanized." She pauses. "Or you can come with us, Nano, right now. That way the dogs will definitely live. I promise that. They'll live. Jack probably won't though. I hope you understand, I can't allow dissent. We simply have too much at stake here."

Finally I turn to look at her. But she turns around, too, and begins to walk away, her tail bobbing up and down with every step.

The people in dog suits follow, passing me in silence.

Mom rushes over and kisses the top of my head, then pulls away.

"Are you really going to go? You're going to leave us here?" I shout.

"I have no choice," Mom sobs. "There are three of them. They have a knife. They have Kinderend. They will kill me, and you, and Jack, and everyone if I don't go."

I watch Mom run after Dorothy. I imagine her tackling Dorothy to the ground.

She doesn't. Through the path we left in the brush, I see that they return to the GoPod and drive away.

So that's it. I'm alone now. I race to Jack. He lies injured on the ground, his hands still behind him. They are tied up with some kind of plastic cord that I can't tear through. I call my robot dog Billy over to try to bite through it. I guess he doesn't understand what I am ordering him to do, though. I tell him to go get the *knife* but he still doesn't move. He really is just for *companionship*, I think. It's a great function, but a bad time to learn his limitations.

I can hear the dogs howling. It doesn't sound far away.

"Jack, we have to get out of here," I say to him. "Can you walk?"

He shakes his head no. "You can leave without me," he says.

"Stop talking like this," I beg. "Let's go. We have to get out of here."

He sits still on the ground. There's a lot of blood. I didn't realize how deeply he'd been stabbed.

The dogs are coming closer. I can now hear their movement through the jungle. Two appear, then three more. One of them is Donut's mom. Red and beautiful. They stride toward us, closer, closer, closer. Their heads hang low, their necks stretched out. I have one can of Kinderend.

Billy, my robot dog, begins to run at them, even just with his three legs. He bares his teeth. He snaps. They retreat, but not far.

Holding out the canister, I begin yelling, "Raah, raah, raah!" Billy keeps after the dogs as they get nearer. At first that works to scare them off, but then they seem to get used to him, and they take turns coming in to sniff his butt (which must be confusing, since it probably smells like metal and not like dog). Then three dogs come toward us at once. Then a fourth. A fifth. Their mouths hang open, slightly. Their ears are pinned forward. I yell at them to go go go go go go go. I tell them that I have the Kinderend.

Jack is moaning. He is crying. He begs me to use the Kinderend on him. He doesn't want to be ripped apart by the dogs, the dogs he grew up worshipping. He cries that he has nothing left.

"What about your mother?" I say. "You can't leave her. You can't leave *me*."

"What's the difference," he says back. "We're all going to die, anyway. Let me do it now. Please. End my suffering."

I tell him to shut up, hold on. Let's get through this, let's at least try.

The dogs form a circle around me and Jack and Billy. And then they sit, very still.

It is clear. They are not going to hurt us. They are guarding us.

"Jack," I say. "Jack, look."

He raises his head. He looks at them, then at me. He smiles.

JACK IS TOO INJURED to walk, and I can't lift him. There's no choice but for him to remain behind there, in the Ruffuge. I trust that he will be protected. I have to trust that he will be protected. I leave him the Kinderend in case not. I ask Billy to stay with him, too, but he follows me anyway.

It's too dangerous to go back to the gate. So I walk to the fence, climb it, and swim back to Dog Island, as fast as I can.

Billy can't climb. He can't come. I have to trust he will be okay, too.

Back on shore, sopping wet, I begin to make my way toward the Dog Island workshop, where all our tools and whatnot are kept. I'll find a bolt cutter to cut Jack loose, I figure, then grab a kayak. Then get back to the Ruffuge. Somehow I'll cut through the electric fence, get Jack onto the kayak. Paddle us both home.

Then . . . who the hell knows. My robot dog Billy won't be able to come because he isn't waterproof on a good day, and this is not a good day. Well, I'll find a way to come back to get him, too. No way am I ditching him again. He's a robot sure, but he's family now. I will find a *way* to keep him safe, from the water, from Mechanical Tail, from anything that tries to take him.

As I'm walking, wet, hungry, determined, a GoPod pulls up beside me. The door opens. It's Patricia.

"Get in," she says.

I shake my head, my legs wobbly. This is the end. "I . . . Jack—"

"I know," she says, exasperatedly. "We are the Underdog Tailroad. The Bad Bitches want to help, Nano."

Collapsing into the GoPod, I have no choice but to pray to Dog that Patricia is being honest. Her robot dog Sasha is in the vehicle, too, in the back seat. Another voice comes through Sasha's mouth: "We are ready. Do you have the biscuit?"

Patricia shouts, "Bitches: I have the biscuit!" She turns to me, "That's you."

"Can they hear you?" I ask.

"I think so," she says. "I think this is one of the models with two-way. But I'm never really sure. I'm not here because I'm great with technology, you know!"

She pets Sasha, and says, "Good girl. Good robot dog."

Patricia starts driving us toward the Ruffuge. I see there's a whole caravan of other GoPods also heading in that direction. Maybe twenty of them. We pull in line at the rear. I feel my heart lift. We pass the Casino, The Smiling Manatee. I wonder if that's where Wolf and Donut are hiding out. I pray to Dog they are safe. Together we bounce along the beach, take a right, plunge down the long, long dirt road—to the gate, en masse.

It doesn't open.

Patricia's GoPod is still at the back of this motley caravan, so I hop out and race toward the security booth, hoping Betsy will let me back in. If not, I think, I will have to go back for the bolt cutters, for the kayak. But that might not be possible. There must be forty people here now. They're getting out of their vehicles. They're forming a crowd.

Either this is going to work now, or . . .

People step aside to let me pass. A few touch my arm. I hear, "You get 'em, Nano" and, "Go on, girl" and, "Dog be with you."

I enter the guardroom. Inside is Betsy. Dorothy is there, too. At first I think that the jig is up. We're done. But then I see that Dorothy is restrained. Now her hands are tied behind her back. She is being guarded by a person in a dog suit. This time the figure looks more familiar. As I stare, the person pulls off his mask, and a cascade of wavy brown hair tumbles out. I see some exceptionally pretty eyes.

Wolf.

"Thank you," Betsy whispers. "Dog bless you. Dog bless you, Nano and Wolf."

"What are you doing here?" I ask him.

Wolf explains that his hiding spot wasn't so good. The Bad Bitches found him, like instantly, and first kissed Donut head to tail, then explained the urgency of the matter. How bad it really was. Jack in the Ruffuge, Dorothy taking out vengeance on dissenters. He couldn't let me face this alone.

I kiss him. Then pull away to ask, "Where is Donut?"

Betsy opens the gate. I go outside. I see Donut in the passenger seat of the first GoPod, waiting by the gate. I reach through the window and grab him out, kissing him and cuddling him and for once he's not trying to wiggle away; he just seems really happy to see me; his tail just wags and wags.

Still holding Donut, I ask the driver of the GoPod—it's Owen, whom I didn't even know was part of this movement— if I can take the wheel. He gets out. I climb into the driver's seat. Wolf races to join me in the passenger seat. Donut goes onto his lap. The first gate opens. Then the second. Then we're inside.

I drive and drive until I find Jack. He is on the ground, bloody and barely hanging on, but he is hanging on. The five dogs are sitting with him.

Billy my robot dog sits with them, too. He found his way back. He wags what's left of his tail so hard when he sees me, I'm worried the last stub will fall off. I'm ridiculously head over heels overjoyed to see him, too.

"Good boy," I tell him. "You are a very good robot dog."

EPILOGUE

It takes Jack several weeks at a hospital in Tampa to recover. It is hit-or-miss for a scary time. But he recovers. He gets well.

Mom and Dad leave Dog Island for a little bit. They stay with Billy at Fuzzy Mansion and then go up to Rhode Island for a spell to see some cousins. They come home to Dog Island after not too long a time, back to the house.

Mom still does spokesperson-ing for the sanctuary. Dad is still in charge of food, which means the meals still aren't what you'd call "fantastic," but we are fed well enough. We are still vegan here. It's still what seems right, for us.

Some Dog Islanders leave for good. Most, like Mom and Dad, stick around. They tell me that all they've ever wanted to do is live with dogs, to protect dogs. Now they get to do that, beyond their wildest dreams.

The dogs live with us now. The five quickly become twelve, then twenty, and then we resume the hormonal birth control. The dogs live inside our homes. They eat with us and walk with us. They make us laugh and keep us company. They have redomesticated themselves. They wanted to be with us, and we want so badly to be with them.

Donut is big now. He is twenty pounds of fur and fun. We go hiking and walking and swimming together every day. My robot dog Billy comes on some walks, but it's hard for him to walk so much now. Robot dogs, especially really battered ones, wear out eventually, too. Mechanical Tail has gone out of business, and there is no one left to repair him. Wolf does his best to keep Billy going, dreaming up ways to repair his body, keep him with me a little longer. There are times I hold my robot dog Billy and cry, knowing the end will be coming. Hopefully, not soon.

Billy may be slowing down a bit. But he is still here. He is still with me. I press the "positive interaction" button several times a day, though there's no one keeping track, since Mechanical Tail closed up shop. I just like doing it. There's a part of me that thinks, even though he's a robot, Billy might like it, too.

My brother Billy is still on the mainland. He now lives with the veterinarian, Dr. Samira King, in Virginia. She gave up her boyfriend for Billy. Boobie McChicken lives with them, too, and is doing "clucking great," Billy likes to tell me. He is back to investigating animal cruelty. And to finding and liberating the caged dogs like the ones we saw in the basement. This time it's a real liberation.

Dr. King—Sammy—treats the animals that Billy finds. Wanda helps them find homes for the animals—the chickens, and the horses, and the goats, and especially the dogs. She helps their new families learn how to care for them properly. These are good homes, with loving people, who treat their

animals well. Then when these animals die, as they eventually will, their people often come to Dog Island and leave
memorials at the chapel. The walls are getting full. We may
have to expand.

Billy tells me that he used to see the world as full of bad
people who would hurt any living creature, any chance they
got. Now, he says, he sees mostly good.

He can do this, we can do this, because Ellie has convinced
her father Marky Barky to continue supporting our work. She
asked for that, as her wedding present, when she and Fiona
got hitched last month. They are young, but they are in love.

They had their wedding at the Casino. The Dog Island
Coco-Nuts played. Mom and Owen decorated with Ellie's
close supervision. Extra toilet paper, the good kind, was
brought in from the mainland.

Donut and Billy were co-ring bearers. Both wagged their
tails all down the aisle. Carol and Hammie were flown in to
be the flower girls. They had massive tulle skirts and everything.

I was a bridesmaid, standing up on the dais along with Wolf
and Jack. The boys wore new Hawaiian shirts. Fiona and Ellie
dressed me up in the most outrageously gorgeous turquoise-
blue dress I've ever seen. It's not even the kind that can be
blow-cleaned. It needs to be washed in real water. Bonnie did
my hair in one of her stiff glamour styles. I think it looked
okay. Marky Barky told me I looked pretty enough for Hol-
lywood. Wolf took me in his arms and danced me away.

Before the big event, Dad spent hours in his Parents' Room
coming up with two signature cocktails. The Mai Tail and the

Puppy Colada. Both were big hits, if "quite derivative," Mom teased. There was a light drizzle on the wedding day. We all considered it to be a hugely auspicious sign.

Dorothy is still here. She lives inside the Ruffuge now. We built her a small house there, with all available comforts. Twice a day, Dog Islanders wearing dog suits come in to bring her food, and tea, and books.

We've been quietly putting out word that she is easing into retirement. That I am taking over as the head of Dog Island, with Wolf and Jack beside me. And I have some new ideas. The drought has ended, and things are starting to bloom.

EFFECTIVE MAR 1, MECHANICAL TAIL IS BEING PUT TO SLEEP. SORRY TO PUT IT SO BLUNTLY, BUT THEM'S THE FACTS.

WE MADE YOU ROBOT DOGS. PERFECT ROBOT DOGS. JUST LIKE ORGANICS, BUT BETTER. AND YOU REPAID US BY KILLING US? MAYBE YOU DON'T DESERVE PERFECTION.

Since we will no longer EXIST, we will no longer be accepting returns on our ROBOT DOG MODELS. However, the GOVERNMENT has declared that they are TOO TOXIC for landfills, so you can't just THROW AWAY the PERFECT BEINGS that we MADE FOR YOU.

DOG ISLAND has generously agreed to accept and care for your unwanted robot dogs. Please send them to ROBOT DOG SANCTUARY PLAN, care of DOG ISLAND, DOG ISLAND, FLORIDA 33700. Postage will be covered, if you call ahead. (Robot) Dog be with you.

ACKNOWLEDGMENTS

First and foremost, thank you to my editor, Dan Ehrenhaft, and publisher, Bronwen Hruska—and a million more thank yous again to everyone at Soho Teen, for treating me and my book so well. Thank you, too, to my agent, Emily Sylvan Kim.

Thank you to my family—the family I was born into and the family I've acquired through marriage. Not to get too sappy here, but I love and appreciate you all very, very much. (Hi, Maxxy Danger from your Auntie Arin!)

With all my heart I want to thank the animal rescuers, the shelter workers, the advocates—the people whose lives are dedicated to helping animals. Your work is so inspiring, and brave, and hard, and important. The world is a better place for animals and people because of what you do.